PENGUIN CLASSICS
Maigret in New York

'I love reading Simenon. He makes me think of Chekhov'
– William Faulkner

'A truly wonderful writer . . . marvellously readable – lucid, simple, absolutely in tune with the world he creates'
– Muriel Spark

'Few writers have ever conveyed with such a sure touch, the bleakness of human life'
– A. N. Wilson

'One of the greatest writers of the twentieth century . . . Simenon was unequalled at making us look inside, though the ability was masked by his brilliance at absorbing us obsessively in his stories'
– *Guardian*

'A novelist who entered his fictional world as if he were part of it'
– Peter Ackroyd

'The greatest of all, the most genuine novelist we have had in literature'
– André Gide

'Superb . . . The most addictive of writers . . . A unique teller of tales'
– *Observer*

'The mysteries of the human personality are revealed in all their disconcerting complexity'
– Anita Brookner

'A writer who, more than any other crime novelist, combined a high literary reputation with popular appeal' – P. D. James

'A supreme writer . . . Unforgettable vividness' – *Independent*

'Compelling, remorseless, brilliant'
– John Gray

'Extraordinary masterpieces of the twentieth century'
– John Banville

ABOUT THE AUTHOR

Georges Simenon was born on 12 February 1903 in Liège, Belgium, and died in 1989 in Lausanne, Switzerland, where he had lived for the latter part of his life. Between 1931 and 1972 he published seventy-five novels and twenty-eight short stories featuring Inspector Maigret.

Simenon always resisted identifying himself with his famous literary character, but acknowledged that they shared an important characteristic:

> My motto, to the extent that I have one, has been noted often enough, and I've always conformed to it. It's the one I've given to old Maigret, who resembles me in certain points . . . 'understand and judge not'.

Penguin is publishing the entire series of Maigret novels.

GEORGES SIMENON

Maigret in New York

Translated by LINDA COVERDALE

PENGUIN BOOKS

PENGUIN CLASSICS

UK | USA | Canada | Ireland | Australia
India | New Zealand | South Africa

Penguin Books is part of the Penguin Random House group of companies
whose addresses can be found at global.penguinrandomhouse.com.

Penguin
Random House
UK

First published in French as *Maigret à New York* by Presses de la Cité 1947
This translation first published 2016

010

Copyright 1947 by Georges Simenon Limited
Translation copyright © Linda Coverdale, 2016
GEORGES SIMENON ® Simenon.tm
MAIGRET ® Georges Simenon Limited
All rights reserved

The moral rights of the author and translator have been asserted

Set in Dante MT Std 12.5/15 pt
Typeset by Palimpsest Book Production Limited, Falkirk, Stirlingshire
Printed and bound in Great Britain by Clays Ltd, Elcograf S.p.A.

ISBN: 978-0-241-20636-2

www.greenpenguin.co.uk

MIX
Paper from
responsible sources
FSC® C018179

Penguin Random House is committed to a
sustainable future for our business, our readers
and our planet. This book is made from Forest
Stewardship Council® certified paper.

Maigret in New York

1.

The ship must have reached the Quarantine Landing at about four in the morning, and most of the passengers were asleep. Some had half-awakened at the loud rattling of the anchor, but in spite of their earlier intentions, very few of them had ventured up on deck to gaze at the lights of New York.

The final hours of the crossing had been the hardest. Even now, in the estuary, a few cable lengths from the Statue of Liberty, a strong swell heaved under the ship . . . It was raining. Or rather, drizzling: a cold dampness that fell all around, soaking everything, making the decks dark and slippery, glistening on the guard rails and metal bulkheads.

As for Maigret, just as the engines fell silent he had put his heavy overcoat on over his pyjamas and gone up on deck, where a few shadows strode this way and that, zigzagging – now high overhead, now way lower down – as the ship pitched at anchor.

Smoking his pipe, he had looked at the lights and the other vessels awaiting the health and customs officials.

He had not seen Jean Maura. Passing his cabin and noticing light under the door, he had almost knocked, but why bother? He had returned to his own cabin to shave. He had swallowed – he would remember this, the way one remembers unimportant details – a mouthful of brandy straight from the bottle Madame Maigret had slipped into his suitcase.

What had happened next? He was fifty-six; this was his first crossing and he was amazed to find himself so lacking in curiosity, so unimpressed by the magnificent view.

The ship was coming to life. Stewards noisily dragged luggage along the corridors as one passenger after another rang for assistance.

When he was ready Maigret went back up on deck. The misty drizzle was turning milky, and the lights were growing dim in that pyramid of concrete Manhattan had set before him.

'You're not angry with me, are you, inspector?'

Maigret had not heard Maura come up to him. The young man was pale, but everyone out on deck that morning looked bleary-eyed and a little ashen.

'Angry with you for what?'

'You know . . . I was too nervous, on edge . . . So when those people asked me to have a drink with them . . .'

All the passengers had drunk too much. It was the final evening; the bar was about to close. The Americans in particular had wanted to enjoy their last chance at the French liqueurs.

Jean Maura, however, was barely nineteen. He had just been through a long period of intense emotional strain and had rapidly become intoxicated, unpleasantly so, growing maudlin and threatening by turns.

Maigret had finally put him to bed towards two in the morning. He'd had to drag him off by force to his cabin, where the boy rounded on him in protest.

'Just because you're the famous Detective Chief Inspector Maigret doesn't mean you can treat me like a child!' he shouted furiously. 'Only one man – you hear me? – only one man on earth has the right to order me around, and that's my father . . .'

Now he was ashamed, feeling upset and queasy, and it fell to Maigret to buck him up, to clap a hearty hand on his shoulder.

'I went through the same thing well before you did, young man.'

'I behaved badly, I was unfair. You understand, I kept thinking about my father . . .'

'Of course.'

'I'm so glad to be seeing him again and to make sure that nothing has happened to him . . .'

Smoking his pipe in the fine drizzle, Maigret watched a grey boat heaving up and down on the swell draw skilfully alongside the gangway ladder. Officials seemed practically to leap aboard, then vanished into the captain's quarters.

Men were opening the holds. The capstans were already revolving. More and more passengers were appearing on deck, and in spite of the poor light, a few of them insisted on taking photographs. Others were exchanging addresses, promising to write, to see one another again. Still others were in the ship's lounges, filling out their customs declarations.

The customs men left, the grey boat pulled away, and two motor-boats arrived alongside with officials from the immigration, police and health departments. Meanwhile, breakfast was served in the dining room.

At what point did Maigret lose track of Jean Maura? That is what he had the most trouble determining later on. He had gone to have a cup of coffee, had then handed out his tips. People he barely knew had shaken his hand. Next he had queued up in the first-class lounge, where a doctor had taken his pulse and checked his tongue while other officials examined his papers.

At one point, out on deck, there was a commotion. Maigret was told that journalists had just come aboard and were taking pictures of a European minister and a film star.

One little thing amused him. He heard a journalist who was going over the passenger list with the purser exclaim (or so he thought, for Maigret's knowledge of English dated back to his schoolboy days): 'Huh! That's the same name as the famous chief inspector of the Police Judiciaire.'

Where was Maura at that moment? Passengers leaning on their elbows at the rail contemplated the Statue of Liberty as the ship moved on, pulled by two tugs.

Small brown boats as crammed with people as subway cars kept passing close to the ship: commuters from Jersey City or Hoboken on their way to work.

'Would you come this way please, Monsieur Maigret?'

The steamer had tied up at the French Line pier, and the passengers were disembarking in single file, anxious to reclaim their luggage in the customs hall.

Where was Jean Maura? Maigret looked for him. Then his name was called again, and he had to disembark. He told himself that he would find the young man down on the pier with all their luggage, since they had the same initials.

There was no feeling of uneasiness in the air, no tension. Maigret felt leaden, tired out by a difficult crossing and by the impression that he had made a mistake in leaving his house in Meung-sur-Loire.

He felt so out of his element! In such moments, he easily turned peevish, and, as he hated crowds and formalities and had a hard time understanding English, his mood was souring rapidly.

Where was Maura? Now he had to search for his keys, for which he inevitably fumbled endlessly through all his pockets until they turned up in the place where they naturally had to be. Even with nothing to declare, he still had to unwrap all the little packages carefully tied up by Madame Maigret, who had never personally had to go through customs.

When it was all over, he caught sight of the purser.

'You haven't see young Maura, have you?'

'He's no longer on board, in any case . . . He isn't here, either. You want me to find out?'

The place was like a train station, but more hectic, with porters banging suitcases into people's legs. The two men looked everywhere for Maura.

'He must have left, Monsieur Maigret. Someone probably came to get him, don't you think?'

Whoever would have come to get him, since no one had been informed of his arrival?

Maigret was obliged to follow the porter who had carried off his luggage. He had no idea what the barman had handed him in the way of small change or what he should give as a tip. He was literally pushed into a yellow cab.

'Hotel St Regis,' he said four or five times before he could make himself understood.

It was perfectly idiotic. He should not have let himself be so affected by that boy. Because he was, after all, only a boy. As for Monsieur d'Hoquélus, Maigret was beginning to wonder if he was any more reliable than the young man.

It was raining. They were driving through a grimy neighbourhood with nauseatingly ugly buildings. Was this New York?

Ten days . . . No, it was precisely nine days earlier that Maigret had still been ensconced in his usual spot at the Café du Cheval Blanc, in Meung, where it was also raining, as it happens. It rains on the banks of the Loire just as well as in America. Maigret was playing cards. It was five in the afternoon.

Wasn't he a retired civil servant? Was he not fully enjoying his retirement and the house he had lovingly set up? A house of the kind he had longed for all his life, one of those country houses with the wonderful smell of ripening fruit, new-mown hay, beeswax, not to mention a simmering ragout, and God knows Madame Maigret knew her way around simmering a ragout!

Now and then, with an infuriating little smile, fools would ask him, 'You don't miss it too much, then, Maigret?'

Miss what? The echoing chilly corridors of the Police Judiciaire, the endless investigations, the days and nights spent chasing after some lowlife or other?

So there! He was happy. He did not even read the crime reports or more sensational local news items in the newspapers. And whenever Lucas came to see him – Lucas who for fifteen years had been his favourite inspector – it was understood that there would be absolutely no shop talk.

Maigret is playing belote. He bids high-tierce in trump. Just then the waiter comes to tell him he is wanted on the telephone, and off he goes, cards in hand.

'Maigret, is that you?'

His wife. For his wife has never been able to call him by anything but his family name.

'There's someone up from Paris here to see you . . .'

He goes home, of course. In front of his house is parked a well-polished vintage car with a uniformed chauffeur at the wheel. Glancing inside, Maigret thinks he sees an old man with a plaid blanket around him.

He enters his house. As always in such circumstances, Madame Maigret awaits him by the door.

'It's a young man,' she whispers. 'I put him in the sitting room. There's an elderly gentleman in the car, his father, perhaps. I wanted him to ask the man inside, but he said I shouldn't bother . . .'

And that is how, stupidly, while cosily playing cards, one lets oneself be shipped off to America!

Always the same song and dance to begin with, the same nervousness, the clenched fists, the darting sidelong glances . . .

'I'm familiar with most of your cases . . . I know you're the only man who . . . and that . . .' and blah blah blah.

People always think their predicament is the most extraordinary drama in the world.

'I'm just a young man . . . You'll probably laugh at me . . .'

Convinced they will be laughed at, they all find their situation so singular that no one else will ever understand it.

'My name is Jean Maura. I'm a law student. My father is John Maura.'

So what? You'd swear he thinks the whole universe should recognize that name.

'John Maura, of New York.'

Puffing on his pipe, Maigret grunts.

'His name is often in the papers. He's a very wealthy man, well known in America. Forgive me for telling you this, but it's necessary, so that you'll understand . . .'

And he starts telling a complicated story. To a yawning Maigret, who couldn't care less, who is still thinking about his card game and who automatically pours himself a glass of brandy. Madame Maigret can be heard moving around in the kitchen. The cat rubs against the inspector's legs. Glimpsed through the curtains, the old man seems to be dozing in the back of the car.

'My father and I, you see, we're not like other fathers and sons. I'm all he has in the world. I'm all that counts. Busy though he is, he writes me a long letter every week. And every year, during the holidays, we spend two or three months together in Italy, Greece, Egypt, India . . . I've brought you his latest letters so that you'll understand. They're typewritten, but don't assume from this that they were dictated. As a rule my father composes his personal letters on a small portable typewriter.'

'"*My dear . . .*"'

One might almost use such a tone with a beloved woman. The American papa worries about everything, about his son's health, his sleep, his outings, his moods, indeed even his dreams. He is delighted about the coming holidays: where shall the two of them go this year?

The tone is quite affectionate, both maternal and wheedling.

'I'd like to convince you that I'm not a high-strung boy who imagines things. For about six months, something serious has been going on, I'm sure of this, although I don't know what it is. I get the feeling that my father is afraid, that he's no longer the same, that he's aware of some danger.

'I should add that the way he lives has suddenly changed. For months now he has travelled constantly, from Mexico to California and on to Canada at such a hectic pace that I feel this is some sort of nightmare.

'I was sure you wouldn't believe me . . . I've underlined each passage in his letters where he writes of the future with a kind of implicit terror.

'You'll see that certain words crop up again and again, words he never used before.

'"*If you should find yourself on your own . . .*"

'"*If I were to be lost to you . . .*"

'"*When you will be alone . . .*"

'"*When I am no longer there . . .*"

'These words recur more and more frequently, as if they

haunt him, yet I know my father has an iron constitution. I cabled his doctor for reassurance; I have his reply. He makes fun of me and assures me that, barring some accident, my father has a good thirty years ahead of him.

'Do you understand?'

It's what they all say: *Do you understand?*

'I went to see my legal adviser, Monsieur d'Hoquélus, whom you doubtless know by reputation. He's an old man, as you know, a man of experience. I showed him these latest letters . . . I saw that he was almost as worried as I was.

'And yesterday he confided in me that my father had instructed him to carry out some inexplicable transactions.

'Monsieur d'Hoquélus is my father's agent in France, a man he relies on. He is the one who was authorized to give me all the money I might need. Well, recently my father has told him to make lifetime gifts of considerable sums to various people.

'Not in order to disinherit me – believe me, on the contrary: according to signed but not notarized contracts, these sums will be handed over to me in the future.

'Why, when I am his sole heir?

'Because he is afraid, don't you see, that his fortune may not be passed on to me in the proper manner.

'I've brought Monsieur d'Hoquélus with me. He's in the car. If you would like to speak to him . . .'

How could anyone not be impressed by the gravity of the old notary? And he says almost the same things as the young man.

'I am convinced,' he begins, weighing his words, 'that some important event has occurred in the life of Joachim Maura.'

'Why do you call him Joachim?'

'It is his real first name. In the United States, he adopted the more common name of John. And I, too, am certain that he feels he is in serious danger. When Jean admitted to me that he intended to go over there, I did not venture to dissuade him but I did advise him to go accompanied by a person of some experience . . .'

'Why not yourself?'

'Because of my age, first of all. And then for reasons which you will perhaps understand later on . . . I am confident that what is required in New York is a man familiar with police matters. I will add that my instructions have always been to give Jean Maura whatever money he might want and that in the present circumstances, I can only approve his desire to . . .'

The conversation had lasted for two hours, in hushed voices, and Monsieur d'Hoquélus had not been indifferent to the appeal of Maigret's aged brandy. From time to time, the inspector had heard his wife come to listen at the door, not from curiosity, but to find out if she could finally set the table.

After the car had left, what was her amazement when Maigret, none too proud of having let himself be persuaded, had told her bluntly, 'I'm leaving for America.'

'What did you say?'

And now a yellow cab was taking him through unfamiliar streets made depressing by drizzle.

Why had Jean Maura disappeared at the very moment when they reached New York? Was Maigret to believe that he had met someone or that, in his haste to see his father again, he had cavalierly left his companion in the lurch?

The streets were becoming more elegant. The cab stopped at a corner of what Maigret did not yet know was the famous Fifth Avenue, and a doorman hurried over to him.

A fresh quandary about paying the cab driver with this unfamiliar money. Then off to the lobby of the St Regis and the reception desk, where he finally found someone who spoke French.

'I would like to see Mr John Maura.'

'One moment, please . . .'

'Can you tell me if his son has arrived?'

'No one has asked for Mr Maura this morning.'

'Is he in?'

Picking up the receiver, the clerk replied frostily, 'I will ask his secretary.'

'Hello . . . Mr MacGill? . . . This is the front desk . . . There is someone here asking to see Mr Maura . . . What was that? . . . I'll ask him . . . Might I have your name, sir?'

'Maigret.'

'Hello . . . Mr Maigret . . . I see . . . Very well, sir.'

Hanging up, the clerk announced, 'Mr MacGill asked me to tell you that Mr Maura sees people only by appointment. If you wish to write to him and give him your address, he will certainly send you his reply.'

'Would you be kind enough to tell this Mr MacGill that

I have arrived from France expressly to see Mr Maura and that I have important information for him.'

'I am sorry . . . These gentlemen would never forgive me for disturbing them a second time, but if you would take the trouble to write a note here, in the lobby, I will have it sent up with a bellboy.'

Maigret was furious. More with himself than with this MacGill, whom he did not know but had already begun to detest.

Just as he detested, immediately and completely, everything around him: the gilt-encrusted lobby, the bellboys smirking at him, the pretty women coming and going, the cocky men who jostled him without deigning to apologize.

Monsieur,

I have just arrived from France, entrusted with an important mission by your son and M. d'Hoquélus. My time is as precious as yours, so I would be grateful if you would see me right away.

Yours sincerely,

Maigret

For a good quarter of an hour he was left to fume off in his corner, so angry that he smoked his pipe even though he knew this was hardly the place for it. At last a bellboy arrived, who accompanied him up in the elevator, led him along a corridor, knocked on a door and abandoned him.

'Come in!'

Why had he envisioned MacGill as a middle-aged person of forbidding aspect? He was a tall, muscular young man, fashionably dressed, who came towards him holding out his hand.

'Forgive me, sir, but Mr Maura is besieged by so many solicitants of all sorts that we must create a strong barrier around him. You tell me you've just come over from France . . . Am I to understand that you are the . . . the former . . . that is to say . . .'

'The former Detective Chief Inspector Maigret, yes.'

'Please, do sit down. Cigar?'

Several boxes of them were set out on a table. A huge mahogany desk dominated the immense drawing room yet did not make it seem at all like an office.

Disdaining the Havana cigars, Maigret had refilled his pipe and now studied the other man rather coolly.

'You wrote that you've brought us news of Monsieur Jean?'

'If you will allow me, I'll speak personally of that to Monsieur Maura when you've been kind enough to take me to him.'

MacGill showed all his teeth, which were quite beautiful, in a smile.

'It's easy to see, sir, that you are from Europe. Otherwise you would know that John Maura is one of the busiest men in New York, that even I have no idea where he is at this moment and, finally, that I handle all his affairs, including the most personal ones. You may therefore speak candidly and tell me . . .'

'I'll wait until Mr Maura agrees to receive me.'

'He would still have to know what all this is about.'

'I told you, it's about his son.'

'Am I, given your profession, to assume that the young man has done something foolish?'

Unflinching, Maigret continued to stare coldly at the other man.

'Forgive me for insisting, inspector. Although you have retired, according to the newspapers, I suppose that you are still addressed by your title? Forgive me, as I said, for reminding you that we are in the United States, not France, and that John Maura's time is limited. Jean is a charming boy, perhaps a bit too sensitive, but I wonder what he could have . . .'

Maigret calmly rose and picked up the hat he had placed on the rug beside his chair.

'I'll be taking a room in this hotel. When Mr Maura has decided to see me . . .'

'He will not be back in New York for about two weeks.'

'Can you tell me where he is at present?'

'That's hard to say. He travels by plane and was in Panama the day before yesterday. Today he might have landed in Rio or Venezuela . . .'

'Thank you.'

'Do you have friends in New York, inspector?'

'No one besides a few police chiefs with whom I've worked on occasion.'

'Would you allow me to invite you to lunch?'

'I think I would rather have lunch with one of them . . .'

'And if I insisted? I am sorry about the role my position forces me to play and I do hope you won't hold it against me. I'm older than Jean, but not by much, and am quite fond of him. You haven't even given me any news of him . . .'

'Excuse me, but may I know how long you've been Mr Maura's private secretary?'

'About six months. What I mean is, I've been with him for six months but have known him a long time, if not for ever.'

Someone was walking in the next room. Maigret saw MacGill's face change colour. The secretary listened anxiously to the approaching footsteps, watched the gilt knob on the door to the next room slowly turn, then open slightly.

'Come here a moment, Jos . . .'

A thin, nervous face, crowned with hair that was still blond although streaked with white. Eyes that took in Maigret; a forehead folding into a frown. The secretary hurried over, but the new arrival had already changed his mind and entered the office, still staring at Maigret.

'Have we . . . ?' he began, as when one appears to recognize somebody and tries to remember more.

'Detective Chief Inspector Maigret of the Police Judiciaire. More precisely, former Inspector Maigret, as I've been retired for a year now.'

John Maura was shorter than average, lean, but apparently endowed with exceptional energy.

'Is it to me that you wish to speak?'

He turned to MacGill without waiting for a reply.

'What is it, Jos?'

'I don't know, chief . . . The inspector . . .'

'If you wouldn't mind, Mr Maura, I would like to speak to you in private. It's about your son.'

But there was not a single reaction in the face of the man who wrote such affectionate letters.

'You may speak in front of my secretary.'

'Very well . . . Your son is in New York.'

And Maigret's eyes never left the two men. Was he mistaken? He felt distinctly that MacGill was shaken, whereas Maura's sole response was simply to say casually, 'Oh . . .'

'Aren't you surprised?'

'You must know that my son is free to do whatever he likes.'

'Aren't you at least astonished that he hasn't yet come to see you?'

'Given that I don't know when he may have arrived . . .'

'He arrived this morning, with me.'

'In that case, you must know.'

'I know nothing, that's just it. In the rush of disembark-ation and arrival formalities I lost sight of him. The last time I saw and spoke to him was when the ship was anchored at the Quarantine Landing.'

'It's quite possible that he met up with some friends.'

And John Maura slowly lit a long cigar with his initials on the band.

'I'm sorry, inspector, but I do not see how my son's arrival—'

'Has any connection with my visit?'

'That is more or less what I wanted to say. I am very busy this morning. With your permission, I will leave you with my secretary, to whom you may speak freely. Please excuse me, inspector.'

A rather abrupt nod. He turned on his heel and vanished next door. After a moment's hesitation, MacGill murmured, 'With your permission . . .'

And he disappeared in the wake of his employer, closing the door behind him. Maigret was alone in the office, alone and not very proud of himself. He heard whispering in the neighbouring room. He was about to leave angrily when the secretary reappeared, brisk and smiling.

'You see, my dear sir, you were wrong to distrust me.'

'I thought Mr Maura was in Venezuela or Rio . . .'

The young man laughed.

'Back at Quai des Orfèvres, where you had heavy responsibilities, didn't you ever use a little white lie to get rid of a visitor?'

'Thanks anyway for having treated me to the same thing!'

'Come, don't hold a grudge against me . . . What time is it? Eleven thirty . . . If it's all right with you, I'll phone the desk to reserve you a room, otherwise you'd have some difficulty getting one. The St Regis is one of the most exclusive hotels in New York. I'll give you time to take a bath and change, and, if you like, we'll meet at the bar at one o'clock, after which we'll have lunch together.'

Maigret was tempted to refuse and walk out wreathed in his surliest expression. He would have been quite capable, had there been a ship that very evening for Europe, of sailing home without pursuing any closer acquaintance with this city that had welcomed him so harshly.

'Hello . . . Front desk, please . . . Hello, MacGill here. Would you please reserve a suite for a friend of Mr Maura . . . Yes . . . Mr Maigret. Thank you.'

And turning toward the inspector, he asked, 'Do you speak a little English?'

'Like all those who learned it in school and have forgotten it.'

'In that case, you'll sometimes find things difficult at first. Is this your first trip to the United States? . . . I assure you that I will be ready to assist you in any way I can.'

Someone was behind the connecting door, probably John Maura. MacGill knew this, too, but did not seem bothered by it.

'Just follow the bellboy. I'll see you later, inspector. And Jean Maura will have doubtless reappeared in time to have lunch with us. I'll have your luggage brought up to you.'

Another elevator. A sitting room, a bedroom, a bathroom, a porter waiting for his tip, at whom Maigret stared in bafflement because he had rarely been so bewildered – and even humiliated – in his life.

To think that ten days earlier he'd been quietly playing belote with the doctor, the fertilizer dealer and the mayor of Meung in the warm and always rather dimly lit Café du Cheval Blanc!

2.

Surely this red-headed man was some kind of good genie! On 49th Street, a few steps from the lights and racket of Broadway, he had gone down several stairs as if heading for a cellar and pushed open a door, the window of which had a curtain with little red checks. Those same democratic red checks, so reminiscent of the humble bistros of Montmartre and the Parisian suburbs, reappeared on the tables – and there as well were the zinc-sheathed bar, a familiar smell of cooking and a plumpish *patronne*, a touch provincial, who came over in welcome.

'What will you have to eat, my dears? There's always steak, of course, but today I have such a coq au vin . . .'

The genie or, rather, Special Agent O'Brien, smiled very sweetly, almost bashfully.

'You see?' he said to Maigret, not without a touch of irony. 'New York is not what people think.'

And soon an authentic Beaujolais stood on the table to accompany the steaming plates of coq au vin.

'You're not going to tell me, O'Brien, that Americans are used to . . .'

'Eating the way we are this evening? Perhaps not every day. Perhaps not everyone. But believe me, some of us do not turn up our noses at classic cookery, and I'll find you a hundred restaurants like this one. You arrived this morning, and barely twelve hours later here you are right at home, aren't you? . . . Now go on with your story.'

'This MacGill, as I mentioned, was waiting for me at the bar in the St Regis. I could tell immediately that he'd decided to change his attitude towards me.'

MacGill had stuck to him all afternoon, and it was only after shaking him off that Maigret had been able at six o'clock to call Special Agent O'Brien of the FBI, whom he had met in France a few years earlier while involved in a major international case.

No creature could have been gentler, more placid than this tall redhead with a sheepish expression, a man so shy that at the age of forty-six he still blushed. He had told Maigret to meet him in the St Regis lobby, but after the inspector mentioned John Maura, O'Brien had first taken his colleague to a small bar near Broadway.

'I suppose you don't like whisky or cocktails?'

'I admit that if there's any beer around . . .'

It was a bar like any other. A few men at the counter; lovebirds at the four or five tables bathed in shadows. Wasn't it a strange idea to have brought him to a place where he clearly didn't fit in?

And wasn't it stranger yet to see O'Brien select a coin from his pocket and slip it solemnly into the slot of a juke-box that began softly to play a sappy, sentimental melody?

And the redhead smiled, considering his colleague with a twinkling eye.

'You don't like music?'

Maigret hadn't had time yet to work off all his ill humour and could not help letting it show.

'All right. I won't keep you in suspense. You see that jukebox cranking out music? I've just put a five-cent piece, a nickel, in the slot, which buys me about a minute and a half of some tune or other. There are a few thousand machines of this kind in the bars, taverns and restaurants of New York. There are tens of thousands in the other cities of America and even way out in the countryside. At this very moment, while we're talking, at least half of these machines you find rather vulgar are in use, meaning people are all putting in their nickels, which makes thousands and thousands of times five cents, which makes . . . Well, I'm not real good at math.

'And do you know to whom all these nickels go? To your friend John Maura, better known in this country as Little John, on account of he's short.

'And Little John has installed the same machines, on which he's basically got a monopoly, in most of the South American republics.

'Now do you understand why Little John is a very important person?'

Always that barely perceptible sting of irony, so that Maigret, unused to this tone, was still wondering whether O'Brien was naive or poking fun at him.

'Now we can go have dinner, and you'll tell me your story.'

Sitting at their table, they were nice and warm, while the wind gusted so fiercely outdoors that passers-by walked leaning forwards, people chased after their hats, and women had to hold their skirts down with both hands. A storm, doubtless the same one Maigret had weathered at sea, had hit the east coast, and New York was taking a beating: storefront signs tore loose from time to time, things fell from high buildings and even the yellow cabs seemed to struggle as they ploughed through the wind.

The bad weather had begun right after lunch, when Maigret and MacGill had left the St Regis.

'Do you know Maura's secretary?' the inspector now asked O'Brien.

'Not particularly. You see, my dear inspector, our rules here are not exactly the same as yours. I regret this, incidentally, because it would make our job much easier. We have a highly developed sense of personal freedom, and if I were to start asking questions about a man, even discreetly, without any grounds for suspicion, I'd find myself in a very awkward situation.

'Now, Little John, let me hasten to add, is not a gangster. He is a well-considered and considerable businessman who maintains a sumptuous suite year-round at the St Regis, one of our best hotels.

'We therefore have no reason to pay attention to him or his secretary.'

Why that vague yet mocking smile that seemed somehow to qualify what he said? Maigret found it a little irritating. He felt like a foreigner and, like every foreigner, he easily imagined that he was a figure of fun.

'I don't read detective stories and I don't expect to find America peopled with gangsters,' he replied crossly.

'To get back to this MacGill, who is probably of French origin, I feel, in spite of his name . . .'

And again, the other man, with his exasperating mildness: 'It's difficult, in New York, to untangle people's roots!'

'As I was saying: from the aperitif on, he made every effort to appear as attentive as he had been aloof that morning. He informed me that they'd still had no news from young Maura but that his father was not worried yet because he assumed that a woman was behind this flit. MacGill then questioned me about the women aboard.

'It so happens that during the crossing Jean Maura did seem smitten by one passenger, a young Chilean woman who'll be leaving for South America tomorrow on a Grace Line ship.'

There were murmurs of French at most of the tables, and the *patronne* went from one customer to another, chatting in a familiar, slightly cheeky way in the delectable accent of Toulouse.

'And how are you, my dears? . . . What do you think of this coq au vin, hmm? And afterwards, if you fancy it, there's mocha cake, homemade . . .'

Lunch had been quite different in the main dining room of the St Regis, where MacGill was constantly greeting people while at the same time paying marked attention to Maigret with his constant chitchat. What was it he had said? . . . That John Maura was a very busy man, rather an eccentric, someone who had a horror of new faces and distrusted everyone.

Why wouldn't he have been surprised that morning when someone like Maigret arrived on his doorstep?

'He doesn't like anyone nosing around his affairs, you

understand? Especially where his family's concerned. Listen! I'm sure that he adores his son, and yet he never says a word about him to me, although I am his closest collaborator . . .'

What was he getting at? It was easy to guess. He was clearly trying to discover why Maigret had sailed across the Atlantic with Jean Maura.

'I had a long conversation with him,' continued MacGill. 'He's instructed me to find out what's happening with his son. I have an appointment soon right here in the hotel with a private detective we've previously employed for minor matters, a top-notch man who knows New York almost as well as you know Paris . . . You can come with us, if you want, and I'd be surprised if we haven't found our boy by this evening.'

All this Maigret was now relating to O'Brien, who listened while enjoying his dinner with somewhat maddening slowness.

'When we left the dining room, a man was indeed waiting for us in the lobby.'

'Do you know his name?'

'He was introduced to me, but I can remember only the first name, Bill . . . Yes, that's it, Bill. I've seen so many people today, whom MacGill all calls by their first names, that I confess I'm a bit lost.'

Still that same smile.

'An American custom, you'll get used to it. What's he like, this Bill?'

'Rather tall, rather heavy . . . About as big as I am. A broken nose and a scar across his chin.'

O'Brien definitely knew him: his eyelids twitched, but he said nothing.

'We took a cab over to the French Line pier.'

The storm was at its worst. The wind had not yet driven away the rain, which fell on them in gusts each time they stepped out of their cab. Vigorously chewing his gum, Bill led the way, his hat pushed back on his forehead as in old films. In fact, had he ever taken this hat off all afternoon? Probably not. Who knows, maybe he was bald!

He talked to everyone – customs officials, stewards, company employees – with equal familiarity, sitting on the corner of a table or desk, speaking briefly, always with the same drawl. And if Maigret did not understand everything he said, he understood enough to know that it was good work from a real professional.

First, customs . . . Jean Maura's luggage had been claimed. When? They checked the records . . . Shortly before noon . . . No, the bags had not been taken into town by one of the usual delivery companies with offices on the pier . . . So his luggage had gone off by taxi or in a private car.

The person claiming the luggage had been in possession of the keys. Was it Jean Maura in person? Impossible to verify. A few hundred passengers had passed through that morning, and more were still showing up to claim their things.

Next, the purser. It was an odd feeling to go aboard an empty ship, to find it deserted after having known it brimming with excitement, to see it being cleaned stem to stern and readied for another crossing.

No doubt about it: Maura had left the ship and handed in his completed customs forms. At what time? No one remembered. Probably during the initial great rush of departing passengers.

The steward . . . This man recalled perfectly that at around eight in the morning, shortly after the arrival of the police and health authorities, young Maura had given him his tip. And the steward had immediately set his suitcase down near the gangway . . . No, the young man had not been at all nervous. A touch tired. He must have had a headache, because he'd taken an aspirin tablet. The empty bottle had been left on the shelf in the bathroom.

The imperturbable Bill with his exasperating chewing-gum forged on. At the French Line offices on Fifth Avenue, he leaned against the mahogany counter and carefully studied the passenger list.

Then, from a drugstore, he telephoned the harbour police.

Maigret felt that MacGill was growing impatient and trying to hide it, but as their inquiries continued, his increasing tension became obvious.

Something was not adding up, something out of line with what he'd been expecting, because he and Bill occasionally exchanged a quick look.

And now, while the inspector was describing their afternoon's activities to O'Brien, his listener, too, grew more solemn and sometimes froze with his fork in mid-air, forgetting to eat.

'They found the Chilean girl's name on the passenger

list and managed to learn where she was staying before her next sailing. It's a hotel at 66th Street . . . We went there . . . Bill questioned the doorman, the desk clerk, the elevator operators: no one could tell him anything about Jean Maura.

'So then Bill gave the driver the address of a bar near Broadway. On the way there he talked to MacGill too fast for me to understand. I did note the name of the place: the Donkey Bar . . . Why are you smiling?'

'No reason,' replied O'Brien casually. 'In short, considering it's your first visit to New York, you've covered a lot of territory. You've even dropped by the Donkey Bar, which isn't bad at all. And what do you think of it?'

Still that feeling he was being played with, in a friendly way, but played with all the same.

'Right out of an American film,' he grumbled.

A long smoke-filled room, an endless bar with the inevitable stools and multicoloured bottles, a black bartender and a Chinese one, the jukebox, and some machines dispensing cigarettes, roasted peanuts and gum.

Everyone in there knew everyone else or at least seemed to. They were all hailing one another as Bob, or Dick, or Tom or Tony and the two or three women were as clearly at home there as the men.

'It appears,' said Maigret, 'to be a gathering place for various journalists and theatre people . . .'

And his companion murmured with a smile, 'You could say that . . .'

'Our detective wanted to speak to a reporter he knows who covers ship arrivals and must have gone aboard this morning. We did find him, in fact: dead drunk or as good as . . . A habit of his, I was assured, after three or four in the afternoon.'

'You know his name?'

'Vaguely . . . Something like Parson . . . Jim Parson, I think it is . . . He has washed-out blond hair, bloodshot eyes and nicotine stains all around his lips.'

Agent O'Brien could claim all he wanted that the American authorities had no right to pay attention to anyone whose conscience was clear, but it was still curious how at each name, each new description Maigret brought up, the redhead seemed to know exactly whom he meant.

And so the inspector could not help remarking, 'Are you sure your police here are that different from ours?'

'Very! Now, what did Jim say?'

'I could only understand bits and pieces . . . Drunk though he was, he definitely seemed interested. I should mention that the detective had backed him into a corner and was giving him what for, as the saying goes, pinning him right to the wall. The other fellow was making promises, trying to remember . . . Then he staggered into the telephone booth, and I saw him through the window ask for four separate numbers.

'Meanwhile, MacGill was explaining to me, "You understand, the reporters who went on board still represent our best chance to learn something. Those people are highly observant. They know everybody . . ."

'That's as may be,' continued the inspector, 'but Jim Parson came out of the booth empty-handed and made a beeline for a double whisky.

'He's supposed to keep making inquiries. If he's doing it in bars, he must have passed out by now, because I've never seen anyone go through drinks at that pace.'

'You'll see more like that . . . Well, if I've got it right, this afternoon Jos MacGill seemed to you mighty eager to locate his boss's son.'

'Whereas this morning, he couldn't have cared less.'

O'Brien was fairly worried after all.

'What are you planning on doing?' he asked.

'I admit I wouldn't mind finding the boy . . .'

'And you're not the only one, it seems.'

'You've got an idea, haven't you?'

'I remember, my dear inspector, something you said to me in Paris, during one of our conversations at the Brasserie Dauphine . . . Do you recall?'

'Our conversations, yes, but not whichever remark you're thinking of.'

'I was asking you almost the same question you just asked me, and you puffed on your pipe while you replied, "Me, I never have ideas."'

'Well, my dear Maigret, if you'll allow me to call you that, at this moment, at least, I am like you, which proves that police all over the world have certain things in common.

'I know nothing. I don't know anything – or hardly anything, only what everyone else does – about Little John's affairs or his entourage.

'I didn't even know he had a son.

'And what's more, I belong to the FBI, which handles only certain clearly defined crimes. In other words, if I were unfortunate enough to stick my nose into this business, I'd stand a good chance of being severely reprimanded.

'I don't suppose that what you want from me is advice, right?'

'No,' muttered Maigret, lighting his pipe.

'Because, if it were advice you were after, I'd tell you this.

'The winters in New York are hard on my wife, who's in Florida at the moment . . . As for my son, he's off at college, and my daughter got married two years ago. So I'm on my own. I therefore have a certain number of evenings free. Allow me to put them at your disposal by showing you around a little of New York the way you once showed me around Paris.

'As for that other matter, well . . . How did you put it again? Wait . . . No, don't tell me . . . I've kept a few of your expressions in mind and often repeat them to my colleagues . . . Ah! Yes: As for that other matter, *let it go*.

'I know perfectly well you won't do that. So, if you feel like it, you could come by now and then for a chat.

'I can't keep a man like you from asking me questions, can I?

'And there are some questions it's very hard not to answer.

'For example! Look, I'm sure you'd like to see my office . . . I remember yours, with the windows overlooking the Seine. The view from mine is more prosaic: a big black wall and a parking lot.

'Admit it: the Armagnac is excellent and this little bistro, as you folks call it, isn't bad at all.'

As in certain Paris restaurants, they had to compliment the *patronne* (and even the chef, whom she'd fetched from the kitchen), promise to come again, have one last drink and finally sign a somewhat greasy guest book.

A little later the two men piled into a taxi, and O'Brien barked an address at the driver.

They both smoked their pipes in the back seat during a rather long silence. They both happened to open their mouths to speak at the same instant and turned towards each other, smiling at the coincidence.

'What were you going to say?'

'And you?'

'Probably the same thing you were.'

'I was about to say,' the American began, 'that, judging from what you've told me, MacGill did not want you to meet his boss.'

'My thought exactly. Yet I was surprised not to find Little John any more anxious than his secretary to obtain news of his son. You follow me?'

'And then it's MacGill who goes to a lot of trouble – or pretends to – trying to find the young man.'

'And who put himself out on my behalf. He told me he would call by tomorrow morning with any news.'

'Does he know we're having this discussion tonight?'

'I did not mention it to him.'

'He suspects something. Not that you're meeting me, just someone from the police. Given the contacts you've had with the American authorities, that's inevitable . . . And in that case . . .'

'In that case?'

'Nothing . . . Here we are.'

They entered a large building and a few moments later emerged from an elevator into a corridor with numbered doors. O'Brien unlocked one and switched on the light.

'Sit down . . . I'll show you around the premises another time because right now you wouldn't see the place at its best. Will you forgive me if I leave you on your own for a few minutes?'

Those few minutes turned into a long quarter of an hour, during which Maigret found himself thinking of nothing but Little John. It was odd: he'd seen the man for only a few brief moments. Their conversation had been, in fact, fairly banal. Nevertheless, as the inspector was suddenly realizing, Maura had made a strong impression on him.

He could still see him: short, thin, dressed almost too correctly. There was nothing special about his face. So what was it about him that had struck Maigret so forcefully?

He was intrigued. He concentrated on remembering, recalled the slightest actions of the lean and tense little man.

And he abruptly remembered his gaze, his first look above all, when Maura had not yet known that he was being observed, as he half-opened the door to the other room.

Little John had cold eyes!

Maigret would have been hard put to explain what he meant by that, but he knew it nonetheless. Four or five times in his life, he had met people with cold eyes, those eyes

that can stare at you without establishing any human contact, without giving any sense of the universal human
need to communicate with one's fellow man.

The inspector had come to speak to the man about his
son, this boy to whom he sent letters as tender as love
notes, and Little John was observing him without any
curiosity or emotion, as if he were looking at a chair or
a stain on the wall.

'You're not annoyed that I left you alone so long?'

'No, because I think I've just discovered something.'

'Ah!'

'I've just discovered that Little John has cold eyes . . .'

Maigret was expecting another smile from his American colleague. He was almost aggressively anticipating
it, that smile. Agent O'Brien, however, looked at him
thoughtfully.

'That's awkward . . .' he said slowly.

And it was as if they had had a long conversation. Suddenly there was something between them that resembled
a shared uneasiness. O'Brien held out a can of tobacco.

'I prefer mine, thanks all the same.'

They lit their pipes and fell silent once again. O'Brien's
office was ordinary and rather bare. Only the smoke from
the two pipes gave the place any feeling of intimacy.

'I suppose that after your eventful crossing you must be
tired and are no doubt looking forward to bed?'

'Because you would have suggested a different scenario?'

'Oh, just that we go and have a nightcap . . . in other
words, one last whisky.'

Why had he taken the trouble to bring Maigret to his

office, where he'd simply left him alone for a quarter of an hour?

'Don't you find it rather cold in here?'

'Let's go wherever you like.'

'I'll drop you off near your hotel . . . No, I won't come in; the front desk staff would start to worry if they saw me show up . . . But I do know a little bar . . .'

Another little bar, with a jukebox in a corner and a line of solitary men leaning on the bar, drinking with stubborn concentration.

'Try a whisky anyway, before bed. You'll see, it's not as bad as you think . . . and it has the advantage of getting the kidneys working . . . By the way . . .'

Maigret understood that O'Brien was finally getting to the point of this last nocturnal ramble.

'Can you imagine, outside my office a little while ago, I bumped into a colleague – and what do you know, he started talking about Little John.

'Mind you, he's never had a thing to do with him, officially . . . Not this colleague, not any of us. You understand? I can assure you that respect for personal freedom is a beautiful thing . . . When you've understood that, you'll be real close to understanding America and its people.

'Look: a man arrives here, a foreigner, an immigrant. You Europeans, you take offence or make fun of us because we make him answer a bunch of written questions, because we want to know, for example, if he has mental problems or has come to the United States intending to assassinate the president.

'We require that he sign this document you find so laughable.

'Afterwards, however, we ask nothing more of him. The formalities for entering the US have perhaps been lengthy and meddlesome, but when they're over, at least our man is home free.

'You get it?

'So free that unless he kills, rapes, or steals, we have no further right to pay any attention to him.

'What was I saying again? . . .'

There were moments when Maigret could have hit him. That fake candour, that nuanced sense of humour he felt incapable of ever figuring out completely . . .

'Oh, yes . . . For example. In fact it was that same colleague, while we were washing our hands, who was telling me this story. Thirty years ago, two men got off a boat from Europe, the way you did this morning. In those days, a lot more of them came over than do today, because we needed workers. They came over in the ships' holds, on the decks . . . They were mostly from Central and Eastern Europe. Some were so filthy and vermin-ridden that our immigration services had to hose them down . . . I bet you'll have another nightcap?'

Too interested to even think of saying no, Maigret simply refilled his pipe and sat back a little because the fellow on his left kept elbowing his ribs.

'The point is, there were all kinds of them who came. And they met with different fates. Today some of them are Hollywood moguls. You'll find a few in Sing-Sing but also in government offices in Washington. You must admit we're really a great country to absorb everyone who comes along the way we do.'

Was it the whisky? Maigret was beginning to see John Maura no longer as a wilful and brusque little man, but as a symbol of the American assimilation of which his companion was speaking in a slow, soft voice.

'So as my friend was telling me . . .'

Did he have three, four whiskies? They had already had some Armagnac, and before the Armagnac two bottles of Beaujolais, and before the Beaujolais a certain number of aperitifs . . .

'J and J . . .'

That was what he remembered most clearly when he finally collapsed into bed in his too-sumptuous suite at the St Regis.

Two Frenchmen, at a time when men wore stiff detachable wing collars, starched cuffs and patent-leather shoes . . . Two very young Frenchmen, greenhorns fresh off the boat without a cent, full of hope, one with a violin under his arm, the other with a clarinet.

Which of them had a clarinet? He couldn't remember any more. O'Brien had told him, O'Brien with his sheepish smile yet as mischievous as a monkey.

The violin, that must have been Maura.

And both were from Bayonne or thereabouts. And both were around twenty years old.

And they had signed a declaration regarding the president of the United States, whom they promised not to assassinate.

Funny man, that Agent O'Brien, taking him to a little

bar to tell him all this as if he himself had nothing to do with it and were chatting about things completely unconnected to his job.

'The one's name was Joseph, the other's, Joachim. That's what my friend told me. You know, one shouldn't put much trust in stories people tell . . . We in the FBI, we have nothing to do with all that. Those were the days of vaudeville cabarets, what in Paris were known as *cafés-chantants* . . . So to earn a living, even though they were both conservatory graduates, even though they considered themselves great musicians, they put together a comedy act as "J and J": Joseph and Joachim. And both hoped some day to have careers as virtuosi or composers.

'My friend's the one who told me this. It's not important, obviously. Except that I know you're interested in Little John's personality. I'm pretty sure now that he wasn't the clarinet guy . . .

'Bartender . . . The same again . . .'

Was Agent O'Brien drunk?

'J and J,' he repeated. 'Well, my first name is Michael. You know, you can call me Michael. Which doesn't mean that I'll be calling you Jules, because I know that's your first name, but you don't like it . . .'

What else did he say that evening?

'You don't know the Bronx, Maigret. You should get to know the Bronx, it's a fascinating place . . . Not beautiful, but fascinating . . . I didn't have time to drive you there; we're very busy, you know . . . Findlay, 169th Street . . . You'll see, it's a curious neighbourhood. It seems that even today there's still a tailor shop right across the street from the house . . . This is all just talk, just my colleague chatting, and I'm still wondering why he mentioned this to me, since it has nothing to do with us . . . J and J . . . They performed a number, half music, half comedy, in the cabarets and music halls of those days . . . And it would be interesting to find out who played the comic role. Don't you think?'

Perhaps Maigret wasn't used to whisky, but he was even less used to being treated like a child and he was furious when a bellboy escorted him up the stairs at the St Regis, inquiring much too solicitously if he needed anything before retiring.

Another of O'Brien's little jokes, O'Brien with his quiet and terribly ironic smile.

3.

Maigret was asleep at the bottom of a well over the opening of which a red-headed giant was leaning, smiling and smoking an enormous cigar – why a cigar? – when a nasty ringing noise slyly set his face twitching, like a too-smooth lake ruffled by the morning breeze. His entire body heaved twice, from one side to the other, dragging along the covers, and at last an arm reached out to seize the water pitcher at first before the phone was found and a voice growled, 'Hello . . .'

Sitting on his bed, uncomfortably (for he had not had time to adjust the pillow and was obliged to hold the damned phone), he was already – humiliatingly – sure, despite O'Brien's doubtless ironic remarks on the diuretic virtues of whisky, that he had a headache.

'Maigret, yes . . . Who's calling? . . . What?'

It was MacGill, and that wasn't at all agreeable either, to be awakened by this fellow whom he did not care for in the least. Particularly when the other man, aware from his voice that he was still in bed, took the liberty of inquiring brightly, 'A late night, I bet? Did you at least . . . have a pleasant evening?'

Maigret looked around for his watch, which he usually placed on his night table but which was not there. He finally spotted a recessed electric wall clock, and his eyes popped: it said eleven.

'Tell me, inspector . . . I'm calling on behalf of Mr Maura. He would be very glad if you could drop in to see him this morning . . . Any time now, yes . . . I mean, whenever you're ready . . . We'll see you soon. You remember the floor, right? The eighth, all the way at the end of corridor B . . . See you soon.'

He looked everywhere for a bell on a cord by the bed, the kind used in France, to call the maître d', the valet, anyone, but saw nothing like that and for a moment felt lost in his ridiculously large suite. Finally he remembered the telephone and had to request three times, in his semblance of English, 'I would like my breakfast, miss . . . Yes, *breakfast* . . . What? . . . You do not understand? . . . Coffee . . .'

She said something he couldn't quite catch.

'I am asking you for my small lunch!'

He thought she then hung up, but she was transferring him to another line, on which a new voice announced, 'Room service . . .'

It was quite simple, obviously, but only if one knew what to do, and at that instant he was angry at all America for not having had the elementary idea of installing bells on cords in hotel rooms.

To cap it all, he was in the bathtub when someone knocked at the room door and although he kept yelling 'Come in!' the knocking continued. There was nothing for it: dripping wet, he had to put on his dressing gown to go and open the door, because he had locked it. What did the waiter want now? Fine, he had to sign a slip. But now what? The man was still waiting, and at last Maigret realized that he expected a tip. And his clothes were in a heap on the floor!

He was about to explode when, half an hour later, he knocked at John Maura's door. MacGill greeted him, as elegant as always, flawlessly turned out, but the inspector sensed that he had not slept much, either.

'Come in, sit down for a moment . . . I'll tell him you're here.'

He seemed preoccupied. He wasn't bothering to be amiable. Paying no attention to Maigret, he walked into the next room without closing the door behind him.

The second room was a sitting room, which he crossed. Then came a very large bedroom. And still MacGill kept going, to knock at one last door. Maigret hadn't time to see very well. What struck him, though, after the series of luxurious rooms, was how bare the last one looked. And it was later in particular that he realized this, trying to reconstruct the sight he'd had an instant before his eyes.

He would have sworn that the bedroom the secretary entered at the end looked more like a servant's room than a St Regis hotel room. Wasn't Little John sitting at a simple pine table and was it not an iron bedstead that Maigret glimpsed behind him?

A few words exchanged in low tones, and the two men came towards him one behind the other, Little John still tense, his movements deliberate, seemingly filled with prodigious energy he was forced to hold in reserve.

Entering the office, like his secretary he was none too welcoming, and this time it did not occur to him to offer his visitor one of those famous cigars.

He went to sit at the mahogany table in the chair MacGill had been occupying, while the latter casually sat down in an armchair and crossed his legs.

'I am sorry, inspector, to have bothered you, but I thought that we should talk.'

Little John looked up at last at Maigret with eyes that expressed nothing, neither sympathy, nor antipathy, nor impatience. His slender hand, astonishingly white for a man, fiddled with a tortoise-shell letter opener.

He was wearing a navy-blue suit of English cut, a dark tie with a white shirt. His clothes set off his defined yet delicate features, and Maigret noticed that it would have been difficult to tell his age.

'I suppose you've had no news of my son?'

He did not expect a reply and spoke on in a neutral voice, as if to an underling.

'When you came to see me yesterday, I was not interested enough to ask you certain questions. If I've understood correctly, you came over from France with Jean and indicated that it was my son who asked you to make this crossing.'

MacGill was puffing on a cigarette and calmly watching the smoke rise towards the ceiling. Little John was still toying with the letter opener, staring as if unseeing at Maigret.

'I do not think you opened a private detective agency after leaving the Police Judiciaire. On the other hand, given what is widely known of your character, I find it hard to believe that you would have embarked on such an adventure lightly. I suppose, inspector, that you follow me? We are free men in a free country. Yesterday you gained admittance here to speak to me of my son. That same evening, you contacted a member of the FBI to obtain information about me.'

In other words, these two men were already aware of his comings and goings and his meeting with O'Brien. Had they had him followed?

'Allow me to ask you a first question: under what pretext did my son request your assistance?'

And as Maigret made no reply, while MacGill seemed to smile with a note of irony, Little John continued, tense and cutting.

'Retired inspectors do not usually chaperone young people when they travel. I am asking you again: what did my son tell you to make you decide to leave France and cross the Atlantic with him?'

Was he not speaking contemptuously on purpose, hoping thereby to make Maigret lose his temper?

Except that Maigret grew calmer and more imperturbable as the other man spoke. More lucid, too.

So lucid – and this showed so clearly in his gaze – that the movements of the hand holding the letter opener became abrupt and awkward. MacGill, who had turned his head towards the inspector, forgot his cigarette and waited.

'If you will allow me, I will reply to your question with another question. Do you know where your son is?'

'I do not, and that is not what is at issue at this moment. My son is at liberty to do as he pleases, do you understand?'

'So, you know where he is.'

It was MacGill who gave a start and turned quickly to Little John with a hard look in his eyes.

'I tell you again that I know nothing about it and that it is no concern of yours.'

'In that case, we have nothing more to say to each other.'

'One moment . . .'

The little man had leaped to his feet and, still holding the letter opener, had darted between Maigret and the door.

'You seem to forget, inspector, that you are here in a way at my expense. My son is a minor; I assume that he did not let you travel at his request yet at your own expense . . .'

Why did MacGill seem so angry at his boss? He was clearly unhappy with the turn things had taken. And what's more, he did not hesitate to intervene.

'I believe the problem lies elsewhere and that you are offending the inspector to no purpose.'

Maigret saw the look the men exchanged and, although unable to read it on the spot, resolved to decipher its meaning later.

'Obviously,' continued MacGill, who rose in turn and

paced up and down the room more calmly than Little John, 'obviously your son, for some reason unknown to us, although perhaps not to you . . .'

Wait a minute! He was making such a serious insinuation to his boss?

'. . . felt compelled to appeal to someone known for his wisdom in criminal matters . . .'

Maigret remained seated. It was instructive to watch the two of them, so different one from the other. Almost as if, at moments, the contest were playing out between the two of them and not with Maigret.

For Little John, so brusque at first, allowed his secretary, a man thirty years younger, to go on talking. And he did not seem happy about it. He was humiliated, that was clear. He was yielding the floor with regret.

'Given that your son cares about one person and only one, his father; given that he rushed to New York without telling you beforehand – at least so I suppose . . .'

The hit went home, no doubt about it.

'. . . then there is every reason to believe that he heard some upsetting news about you. The question is, who planted this troubling possibility in his mind! Do you not think, inspector, that the entire problem lies there? Let's summarize the matter as simply as possible. You are alarmed by the rather inexplicable disappearance of a young man the moment he arrives in New York. Unfamiliar with police matters and relying solely on common sense, I put it this way.

'When we find out who made Jean Maura come to New York, meaning whoever cabled him who-knows-what about some danger menacing his father (because otherwise, there was no need for him to request the company of a policeman, if I may use that word) – when that has been determined, it should not be hard to discover who made Jean disappear.'

During this lecture, Little John had gone to stand at the window, where, holding the curtain open with one hand, he was gazing outside. His silhouette was as lean of line as his face.

And Maigret found himself wondering: clarinet? Violin? Which of the two Js did this man play in that long-ago burlesque act?

'Am I to understand, inspector, that you refuse to answer?'

Then Maigret, fishing for advantage, announced, 'I would like to speak with Mr Maura in private.'

Little John whipped around, startled. His first glance was for his secretary, who seemed supremely indifferent.

'I have already told you, I think, that you may speak in front of MacGill.'

'In that case, please forgive me if I have nothing to say to you.'

Well, MacGill was not offering to leave. He stayed on, sure of himself, like someone who knows he's in the right place.

Was it the little man who would lose his temper? In his cold eyes there was something like exasperation, but like something else as well.

'Listen to me, Mr Maigret. We must make an end of this and will do it in few words. Talk or don't talk, it's all the same to me, because what you might have to say does not much interest me. A boy, worried for reasons I don't know, went to see you, and you jumped headlong into an affair that did not concern you. This boy is my son. He is a minor. If he has disappeared, that is my business and mine alone, and if I must turn elsewhere to look for him, it will be to the police of this country. I assume I am making myself clear?

'We are not in France and, until further notice, my doings are my own affair. I will therefore allow no one to interfere with me and, if necessary, I will take steps to see that my full and complete liberty will be respected.

'I do not know if my son gave you what's called an advance. If he did not think of it, let me know, and my secretary will hand over a cheque covering your current travel expenses and return passage to France.'

Why did he glance briefly at MacGill as if seeking his approval?

'I am waiting for your answer.'

'To which question?'

'Regarding the cheque.'

'I thank you.'

'One last word, if you please . . . You are entitled, of course, to stay as long as you like in this hotel, where I am simply a guest like any other. I will merely tell you that I would find it extremely unpleasant to encounter you repeatedly in the lobby, the corridors or the elevators . . . I bid you good day, inspector.'

Still seated, Maigret slowly knocked his pipe out in an ashtray on a nearby table. He took the time to pull a fresh pipe from his pocket, then fill and light it while looking from one man to the other.

Finally, he rose, seeming to unfold his height and heft, and he looked taller, larger than usual.

'Goodbye,' was all he said, so unexpectedly that the letter opener snapped clean in two in Little John's hand.

He had the feeling that MacGill wanted to say something further to prevent him from leaving right away, but, calmly turning his back, the inspector walked to the door and on down the corridor.

It was only in the elevator that his headache returned and that the previous evening's whisky came back to him as an upset stomach.

'Hello . . . Agent O'Brien? . . . Maigret here.'

He was smiling. He was smoking his pipe in little puffs as he looked around at the slightly faded wallpaper in his room.

'What? . . . No, I'm not at the St Regis any more . . . Why? Several reasons, the most important being that I wasn't truly comfortable there. You follow me? . . . Good . . . Well of course I've found a hotel. The Berwick . . . You don't know it? I can't remember the street number; I've never had a head for numbers, and you people are a nuisance with your numbered streets, as if you couldn't just say Victor Hugo Street, Pigalle Street or President Whosis Street . . .

'Hello? . . . On Broadway, I don't know how far up, there's a cinema called the Capitol . . . Right. Well, it's the first or second street on the left. A small hotel, nothing fancy, and I suspect they rent out rooms not just for the night . . . Oh, really? It's illegal in New York? Too bad!'

He was in a good mood, even a jolly mood, for no particular reason, perhaps simply because he was back in a familiar atmosphere.

First of all, he liked this noisy and rather vulgar part of Broadway, which reminded him of both Montmartre and the Grands Boulevards of Paris. The reception desk looked almost second-hand, and there was only one elevator. Operated by a little man with a limp!

From the window he could see neon signs blinking on and off.

'Hello? O'Brien? Guess what: I need you again . . . Don't worry, I'm scrupulously respecting all the liberties of America the free . . . What? . . . No, no . . . I assure you, I am completely incapable of irony . . . Imagine this: I, too, would like to engage the services of a private detective.'

At the other end of the line, O'Brien, wondering if he was joking, grunted indistinctly, then decided to burst out laughing.

'Don't laugh, I'm quite serious . . . I actually have a detective at my disposition . . . I mean that since noon, I have one at my heels . . . Not at all, my friend, I'm not accusing the official police . . .Why are you so touchy today? I'm talking about Bill from yesterday . . . Yes, the boxer with the scarred chin who accompanied MacGill and me on our peregrinations . . . Well, he's back, except that he's walking ten metres behind me like an old-fashioned footman . . . If I were to lean out the window,

I'd certainly see him in front of the hotel entrance . . .
He's not trying to hide, no . . . He's following me, that's
all . . . I even think that he's somewhat ill at ease and
sometimes would like to nod hello at me . . .

'What? . . . Why do I want a detective? . . . Laugh all
you want. I admit it's sort of funny. Nevertheless, in your
confounded country, where no one deigns to understand
my English unless I repeat it four or five times complete
with sign language, I wouldn't say no to someone's help
with the few little inquiries I want to make . . .

'Above all, I beg you, your man must speak French! . . .
You have someone available? . . . You'll telephone? . . . Yes,
absolutely, as of this evening . . . I'm in fine fettle, tip-top,
in spite of your whiskies . . . Although I did inaugurate
my new room in the Berwick by treating myself to a two-
hour nap . . .

'In which milieux will I be making my inquiries? I
thought you would have guessed . . . Naturally . . . That's
right . . .

'I'll wait for your call. I'll talk to you soon . . .'

He went to open the window and, as expected, saw the
aforementioned Bill chewing his gum about twenty
metres from the hotel and looking none too happy.

The room was perfectly ordinary, with enough old
things and shabby carpeting to make it resemble a rented
room in any city in the world.

Before ten minutes had passed the telephone rang.
O'Brien announced to Maigret that he'd found him a
detective, one Ronald Dexter, and recommended that he
not let him drink too much.

'Because he can't handle whisky?'

And O'Brien replied with angelic sweetness, 'Because he cries . . .'

The placid redhead was not joking. Even when he hadn't been drinking, Dexter gave the impression of a man who goes through life saddled with immeasurable sorrow.

He arrived at the hotel at seven that evening. Maigret met him in the lobby just as the detective was asking for him at the desk.

'Ronald Dexter?'

'That's me.'

And he seemed to be saying, 'Alas!'

'Has my friend O'Brien brought you up to date?'

'Shh!'

'Excuse me?'

'No last names, please. I am at your service. Where do you want us to go?'

'Outside, to begin with . . . Do you know that gum-chewing gentleman out there with an apparently lively interest in passers-by? That's Bill . . . Bill who? I've no idea. All I've got is his first name, but what I do know is that he's one of your colleagues who's been told to follow me . . . I mention this so that you won't worry about his comings and goings. He can follow us as much as he likes. It's of no importance, you understand?'

Dexter either did or didn't understand. In any case he adopted a resigned expression and seemed to say to heaven above, 'If it's not one thing, it's another!'

He must have been about fifty; his grey clothing and mangy trenchcoat did not plead in favour of prosperity.

The two men walked the hundred metres or so to Broadway, with Bill falling imperturbably in behind them.

'Are you familiar with theatrical folks?'

'Somewhat.'

'More precisely, variety acts, cabarets?'

Then Maigret realized the extent of O'Brien's sense of both humour and practicality, as Dexter sighed, 'I was a clown for twenty years . . .'

'A sad one, no doubt? If you like, we can go to a bar and have a drink.'

'I wouldn't mind.'

Then, with disarming simplicity, 'I thought you'd been warned . . .'

'About what?

'I can't hold my liquor very well. Oh . . . Just one drink, right?'

They sat off in a corner, while Bill came in as well and settled in at the bar.

'If we were in Paris,' Maigret explained, 'I'd find the information I want right away, because around the Porte Saint-Martin area we have shops that date back to another era. Some of them sell popular song sheets, and today you can still find the tunes sung on every street corner in 1900 or 1910 . . . In one place I know, a wigmaker's boutique, you'll see every kind of beard, moustache and wig worn by actors since time immemorial . . . And in some seedy neighbourhoods, the most unlikely impresarios organize tours through small provincial towns . . .'

As Maigret was speaking, Ronald Dexter gazed at his glass with a deeply melancholy eye.

'You see what I mean?'

'Yes, sir.'

'Good. On the walls of such offices, it would not be hard to find posters for vaudeville and cabaret acts from thirty or forty years ago . . . And, sitting on the waiting-room benches, a dozen old ham actors, washed-up comedians or cabaret canaries—'

Breaking off, the inspector said, 'Please forgive me.'

'Not at all.'

'What I mean is, actors, singers, chanteuses now seventy and more who still come looking for work. These people have amazing memories, especially of their glory days. So, Mr Dexter . . .'

'Everyone calls me Ronald.'

'So, I'm wondering if New York has the equivalent of what I just described.'

Still staring at his glass, which he had not yet touched, the former clown took some time to reflect. At last he inquired, with the utmost gravity, 'Must they be really very old?'

'What do you mean?'

'Do they have to be really old performers? You mentioned seventy and up. Around here, that's a lot, because, you see, we die more quickly.'

His hand reached for the glass, drew back, reached out again; finally he downed the drink in one gulp.

'There are places . . . I'll show you.'

'We only have to go back about thirty years. At that time, two Frenchmen billed as J and J performed a musical number in cabarets.'

'Thirty years, you say? I think that's possible. And you'd like to know . . .'

'Everything you can learn about them. I'd also like to obtain a photograph. Performers have lots of pictures taken, images that turn up on posters, in programmes.'

'Do you intend to come with me?'

'Not tonight. Not right away.'

'That would be better. Because, you see . . . you risk scaring people off. They're very sensitive, you know. If you want, I'll come and see you tomorrow at your hotel, or else I'll phone you. Is this quite urgent? I can get started tonight. But I'd need . . .'

He hesitated, lowered his voice.

'I'd need you to pay me enough for a few rounds, to get in a few places.'

Maigret pulled out his wallet.

'Oh! Ten dollars will be enough. Because if you give me more, I'll spend it. And when I've finished your job, I'll have nothing left . . . You don't need me any more, now?'

The inspector shook his head. He had considered for a moment having dinner with his clown, but the fellow was proving to be too hopelessly mournful.

'It doesn't annoy you, having that fellow following you?'

'What would you do if it did?'

'I think that offering him a bit more than his employers are paying would . . .'

'He's not bothering me.'

And it was true. It was almost a diversion for Maigret to feel the former boxer shadowing him.

He dined that evening in a brightly lit cafeteria on Broadway, where he was served excellent sausages but irritated at finding only Coca-Cola in lieu of beer.

Then, towards nine o'clock, he hailed a cab.

'The corner of Findlay and 169th Street.'

The driver sighed, lowering his flag with an air of resignation, and Maigret understood his reaction only a little later, when the taxi left the well-lit neighbourhoods to enter a different world.

Soon, along endless, perfectly straight streets, the only passers-by to be seen were coloured. The cab was crossing Harlem, with its houses all alike, its blocks of dark brick made even uglier by the iron fire escapes zigzagging across the façades.

Much later, they crossed a bridge, passing close to warehouses or factories – it was hard to tell in the darkness – and then, in the Bronx, there were more desolate avenues, sometimes with the yellow, red or violet lights of a neighbourhood cinema, or the display windows of a large store crowded with wax mannequins in rigid poses.

They drove for more than a half an hour, and the streets became yet darker, more deserted, until at last the driver stopped his cab and turned around to announce disdainfully, 'Findlay.'

To the right was 169th Street. But Maigret had to negotiate a long time to persuade the driver to wait. And he still would not wait at the corner, for as Maigret set out along the sidewalk, he crept along behind him. And a second taxi rolled slowly along as well, Bill's cab, no doubt, but the boxer-detective did not bother getting out of his.

In the darkness, one could see the rectangular outline of a few stores like those found in the poor sections of Paris and all capital cities.

What had Maigret come here to do? Nothing definite. Did he even have any idea what he had come to New York to do? And yet, for a few hours now, since the moment he had left the St Regis, actually, he had no longer felt out of his element. The Berwick had already reconciled him to America, perhaps because it smelled like humanity, and now he imagined all the lives huddled in the small cells within these brick cubes, all the scenes unfolding behind the window shades.

Little John had not affected him, emotionally (those weren't exactly the right words), but he was still some kind of a human being, albeit a somewhat artificial, counterfeit one.

MacGill as well, maybe even more so.

And even the young man, Jean Maura, with his fears and the support of Monsieur d'Hoquélus.

And that disappearance at the moment the transatlantic liner finally docked in New York . . .

All that, after all, was unimportant. That's the word Maigret would have used if the red headed O'Brien had been there at that moment, with his faint smile on his pockmarked face.

A passing reflection as he walked along, hands in his pockets, pipe between his teeth. Why is it usually redheads who are pockmarked and why, almost invariably, are they so likeable?

He sniffed. He breathed in the air smelling vaguely of

fuel oil and poverty. Were there any new J-and-Js in a few of those small cells? Surely there were! Some young people barely a few weeks off their boat and who waited, with jaws set, for their glorious hour at the St Regis.

Maigret was looking for a tailor shop. Two taxis followed him like a parade. And in a way this situation was laughable, he knew that.

Once two young men, back when detachable stiff collars and cylindrical cuffs were in fashion (Maigret had had some washable ones, in rubber or rubberized cloth, he still remembered them), two young men had lived on this street, across from a tailor shop.

Well, another young man, a few days ago, had feared for his father's life.

And this young man, with whom Maigret had been talking a few minutes earlier on the deck of their ship, had vanished.

The inspector was searching for the tailor shop. He looked at the windows of these houses, often disfigured by the contemptible iron fire escapes that stopped short above the ground floor.

A clarinet and a violin . . .

Why did he press his nose, the way he'd done as a boy, to the window of one of those stores that sell everything: vegetables, canned goods, sweets? Right next door there was another shop, unlit but without shutters, and through its window, thanks to the gleam from a nearby street lamp, one could see a pressing machine and some suits on hangers.

Arturo Giacomi.

Still following him, the two taxis had halted a few metres away, and neither the drivers nor that thick lump Bill suspected the contact this man in the heavy overcoat, pipe clenched between his teeth, was making as he turned towards the house across the street: contact with two twenty-year-old Frenchmen who had come off a ship a long time ago, one with his violin under his arm, the other with his clarinet.

4.

It was touch and go that morning whether a man lived or died, whether a repellent crime would be committed or no, and this slim margin depended on only a few minutes more or less in how Maigret spent his time.

Unfortunately, he was unaware of this. Throughout his thirty years with the Police Judiciaire it had been his habit, when an investigation did not keep him out at night, of rising at around seven in the morning, and he loved the rather long walk from his home at Boulevard Richard-Lenoir to Quai des Orfèvres.

At heart, despite his active life, he had always been a flâneur. And once retired, in his house in Meung-sur-Loire, he'd been getting up even earlier; in the summer, the sunrise often found him standing out in his garden.

On board the ship as well, he was almost always the first passenger out pacing the deck, while the crew busily swabbed it down and polished the brass railings.

His first morning in New York, however, because he had drunk too much with Agent O'Brien, he got up at eleven.

The second day, in his room at the Berwick, he woke early, as usual. But precisely because it was too early, because he could tell the streets were empty even though the curtains were still closed, he decided to go back to sleep. And he did, deeply. When he opened his eyes again, it was past ten. Why did he behave like those people who have worked all week and whose great joy on Sunday is to laze around? He dawdled. He took for ever to eat his breakfast. He went to the window in his dressing gown to smoke a first pipe and was astonished not to see Bill in the street.

True, the boxer-detective had needed sleep as well. Had he arranged for a replacement? Were there two men relaying each other on Maigret's trail?

He shaved carefully and spent still a little more time organizing his things.

Well, it was on all those particular minutes, wasted so trivially, that a man's life depended.

At the moment when Maigret was going down to the street, there was – strictly speaking – still time. Bill was definitely not there, and the inspector noticed no one who seemed assigned to follow him. An empty cab drove by. He raised his arm automatically. The driver did not see him, and, instead of looking for another cab, Maigret decided to walk for a while.

That is how he discovered Fifth Avenue and its luxury stores. He stopped at their windows, lingered a long time in contemplation of some pipes, then decided to buy one, even though Madame Maigret ordinarily gave him one for special occasions and his birthday.

One more silly, preposterous detail: the pipe was quite expensive. Leaving the store, remembering the taxi fare from the previous evening, Maigret resolved to economize the same amount that morning.

That is why he took the subway, in which he lost considerable time before finding the right corner at Findlay Avenue.

The sky was a hard, luminous grey. The wind was still blowing, but no longer as fiercely. Maigret turned at the corner of 169th Street and immediately sensed disaster.

About two hundred metres down the street a crowd was gathered outside a door and, although he did not know the area well and had seen it only at night, he was almost certain the place was the Italian tailor's shop.

Moreover, everything or almost everything on the street and in the neighbourhood was Italian. The children seen playing on the doorsteps had black hair and those sharp-eyed faces, those long tanned legs of street urchins from Naples or Florence.

The names over most of the shops were Italian, and their windows were full of mortadella sausages, pasta and salt-preserved meats from the shores of the Mediterranean.

. The inspector quickened his pace. Twenty or thirty people were clustered on the tailor's threshold, which a policeman was defending against invasion, and a pack of more or less scruffy brats swarmed around them all.

The whole thing smacked of an accident, a sordid tragedy that explodes abruptly in the street and etches the faces of passers-by with dismay.

'What happened?' he asked a fat man in a bowler hat standing on tiptoe at the back of the crowd.

Although he had used English, the man simply examined him curiously before turning away with a shrug.

Maigret heard snatches of talk, some in English, some in Italian.

'. . . just as he was crossing the street . . .'

'. . . for years and years, every morning at the same time, he'd take his walk . . . Fifteen years now I'm in the neighbourhood and I always saw him . . .'

'. . . his chair's still there . . .'

Through the shop window they could see the steam clothes-press with a suit still laid out on it and, closer, next to the plate glass, a straw-bottomed chair with a rather low seat, the one belonging to old Angelino.

Maigret was beginning to understand. Patiently, with that grace big men have, he worked his way slowly in to the heart of the crowd and pieced together the scattered information he overheard.

It had been at least fifty years since Angelino Giacomi had come from Naples and set himself up in this shop, well before the invention of the steam press. He was practically the patriarch of the street, of the whole neighbourhood, and during municipal elections not a single candidate failed to pay him his respects.

His son Arturo ran the shop now, and this son was almost sixty, himself the father of seven or eight children, most of them married.

In the winter, old Angelino spent his days sitting on that straw-bottomed chair in the front window of the shop, as if part of the display, smoking from morning to night those poorly made Italian cigars of black tobacco that smell so harsh.

And in the spring, just as one sees the swallows return,

everyone up and down the street watched as old Angelino set his chair out on the pavement, next to the door.

Now he was dead, or dying, Maigret did not yet know exactly.

Different versions of his fate swirled around the inspector, but soon an ambulance siren was heard, and a vehicle with a red cross pulled over to the kerb.

The crowd rippled, then parted slowly for two men in white coats, who walked into the shop and out again a few moments later, removing a stretcher on which nothing could be seen but a body beneath a sheet.

The vehicle's rear door closed. A casually dressed man, doubtless Angelino's son, having simply put a jacket on over his work clothes, climbed in next to the driver, and the ambulance pulled away.

'Is he dead?' people asked the policeman, still at the door.

He didn't know. He didn't care. It wasn't his job to bother with such details.

A woman was crying inside the shop, with her dishevelled grey hair falling over her face, and sometimes she let out such moans that you could hear her in the street.

One person, two, three decided it was time to leave. Housewives hunted for their youngsters so as to finish their shopping in the neighbourhood.

The crowd was slowly shrinking, but it was still blocking the shop door.

Now it was a barber, comb tucked behind his ear, who was holding forth in a strong Genoese accent.

'I saw everything like I see you, because it's that slow time, and I happened to be right in my doorway.'

And a few houses along, in fact, there was a traditional barber-shop pole striped with red and blue.

'Almost every morning he'd stop a bit outside my place to chat. It's me who shaved him, Wednesdays and Saturdays. I always shaved him. Not my assistant, me personally. And I've always known him to be just as he still was this morning. Though he must have been eighty-two . . . No, wait . . . Eighty-three. When Maria, his last granddaughter, got married four years ago, I remember he told me . . .'

And the barber began calculations to determine the exact age of old Angelino, who had just been brutally taken far away from the street where he had lived for so long.

'There's one thing he would never have let himself admit for the whole wide world: it's that he couldn't see much at all, if anything. He still wore his glasses, thick lenses in old silver frames . . . He passed the time polishing them with his big red handkerchief and putting them back on. But the truth is they didn't help him much . . . That's the reason why – and not that he had bad legs, because he still had the legs of a twenty-year-old – he'd taken to walking with a cane . . .

'Every morning at ten thirty on the dot . . .'

Now, logically, Maigret should have been at his shop around that time. He had promised himself this the night before. Old Angelino was the one he wanted to see and question. What would have happened if Maigret had arrived there on time, if he had not gone back to sleep, if he hadn't dawdled at his room window, if the taxi he hailed had stopped, if he hadn't bought the pipe on Fifth Avenue?

'His folks always tied a thick, knitted woollen scarf around his neck, a red one. A little while ago I saw a boy, the vegetable woman's son, bringing it back to the shop. He never wore an overcoat, not in the worst winter weather. He toddled along with small even steps, sticking close to the houses, and me, I knew his cane helped him find his way . . .'

There were no more than five or six left around the barber, and as Maigret seemed the most seriously interested listener, the man had begun to speak directly to him.

'In front of every shop, or just about, he'd greet people with a wave, because he knew everybody. At the street corner, he'd pause for a moment at the edge of the pavement before crossing, because his walk always covered three blocks . . .

'This morning, he did what he always did. I saw him. I can definitely say I saw him take the first steps into the street . . . Why did I turn around just then? I don't know. Maybe my assistant, back in the shop, called to me through the open door? I'll have to ask him, because I can't figure it out . . .

'I clearly heard the car coming. It happened less than a hundred metres from my place. Then a strange, funny noise, a soft noise . . . It's hard to describe – but in any case, a noise that tells you right away there's been an accident.

'I turned back and I saw the car speeding on its way; it was already passing by me . . . At the same time, I was looking at the body lying there.

'If I hadn't been doing those two things at the same

time, I'd have taken a better look at the two men in the front seat of the car . . . A big grey car. More like a dark grey. I'd almost be tempted to say black, but I think it was grey . . . Or else it was coated with dust.

'People had already rushed over. I came here first to tell Arturo. He was pressing a pair of trousers. They carried old Angelino in with a dribble of blood coming out of his mouth and one arm hanging down, a shoulder of his jacket torn . . . There wasn't anything else to see at first glance, but I knew right away that he was dead.'

They were in the office of Special Agent O'Brien, who, because of his long legs, had tipped his chair back while he took tiny puffs on his pipe, caressing the stem with his lips and watching, with heavy-lidded eyes, as Maigret talked.

'I suppose,' he was saying in conclusion, 'that you won't claim any more that personal freedom prevents you from taking some action against those bastards?'

After more than thirty years of police work, during which he had seen all there was to see of human cruelty, cowardice and depravity, Maigret could still be as infuriated by some things as on his first day in the force.

The concurrence of old Giacomi's death with Maigret's intended visit that morning to the elderly tailor, the fact that this visit, made in time, would probably have saved the man's life, and even that purchase of a pipe he now avoided smoking had all put him in an even darker mood.

'Unfortunately, this matter concerns not the FBI, but the New York police, at least for the time being.'

'They killed him in a lowdown, dirty way,' growled the former inspector.

At which O'Brien murmured pensively, 'It's not so much the way they killed him that strikes me, but the fact that they killed him just in time . . .'

Maigret had already thought about that, and it was hard to see it as a coincidence.

For years and years, no one had paid any attention to old Angelino, who had been able to spend his days on a chair, seen by everyone passing by, and take his usual little morning walk like a good old dog.

Only the previous night, Maigret had stopped for a few moments in front of the tailor's shop. He had resolved, without mentioning this to anyone, to return in the morning to speak to the old fellow.

Yet when he arrived, someone had taken care to make absolutely sure the man would never speak again.

'They had to work fast,' he grumbled, looking at O'Brien with a bitterness he could not hide.

'It doesn't take long to organize that kind of accident when one already knows all the vital details. I wouldn't go so far as to say that there are agencies that handle that sort of job, but it's almost as if there were. In short, it's enough to know whom to contact, to gain their trust, agree on a price . . . and pay it, you understand? They're what are called killers for hire. Only, the killers couldn't have known that old Angelino would cross 169th Street every morning at the same time, at the same place . . .'

'Someone must have told them; in theory, the one who ordered the hit . . .'

'And that person must have known these details for a long time.'

They looked solemnly at each other, for they were both drawing the same conclusions from what had happened.

Someone, for an undetermined length of time, had known that Angelino had something to say, something that threatened his quiet existence.

Maigret could not help thinking of the wiry but almost slight figure of Little John, with his pale, cold eyes devoid of the least flicker of humanity.

Was he not precisely the man capable of hiring killers, without batting an eye, to carry out the assignment they had completed this morning?

And Little John had lived at 169th Street, right across from the tailor's shop!

What's more, if you were to believe his letters to his son – and they had the troubling ring of truth – it was Little John who felt threatened, who no doubt feared for his life!

And it was his son who had disappeared before setting foot on American soil!

'They kill,' said Maigret after a long silence, as if that were the sum of his thoughts.

And that is just about what it was. Moments before, he had mentioned Jean Maura and, now that he knew he was dealing with people capable of murder, he felt remorseful.

Shouldn't he have kept a closer guard on the young man who had asked for his help?

Shouldn't he have taken the boy's fears much more seriously, no matter what Monsieur d'Hoquélus had said?

'In short,' announced the red-headed FBI agent, 'we're

facing people who are defending themselves, or, more precisely, who attack in their own defence. And I wonder, my dear Maigret, what you'll be able to do. The New York police will have no desire to see you get involved in their investigation . . . By what authority, anyway? The crime has been committed on American soil. Angelino has been an American citizen for a long time. As have the murderers, no doubt. Maura is a naturalized citizen . . . I checked: MacGill was born in New York. Anyway, you won't find those two mixed up in this business. As for young Maura . . . No one has filed a complaint, and his father doesn't seem eager to do so.'

He stood up with a sigh.

'That's all I can tell you.'

'Do you know that my bulldog wasn't at his post this morning?'

O'Brien knew he meant Bill.

'You hadn't mentioned that, but I would have bet on it . . . Between last night and this morning, someone had to have been informed of your visit to 169th Street, right?'

'. . . So that from then on I could go back there without any danger to anyone.'

'You know, if I were you, I'd be extra careful about crossing the street . . . And while I was at it, I'd avoid deserted places, particularly in the evening . . . Running people over isn't always necessary . . . It's easy enough to blast them with a machine gun as you drive by.'

'I thought gangsters existed only in pulp novels and films. Isn't that what you told me?'

'I'm not talking about gangsters. I'm giving you some

advice. By the way, what have you done with my melancholy clown?'

'I put him to work, and he's supposed to call me or come to see me at the Berwick today.'

'Unless he has an accident, too.'

'You think so?'

'I don't know a thing. I've no right to get mixed up in anything. I've a good mind to tell you not to either, but it would clearly be useless.'

'True.'

'Good luck. Call me if there's any news. I might just happen to run into whichever of my colleagues in the city police is in charge of this case. I don't yet know who's been assigned to it. It's also possible that, during our conversation, he might tell me a few little things that might interest you. I'm not inviting you to lunch today because I'll be having lunch shortly with two of my superiors.'

It was a far cry from the two men's first meeting and their good-humoured, even joking conversation.

Now they both had heavy hearts. That street up in the Bronx, with its Italian shops, its neighbourly life, the children running around, where an old man toddled along on his walk and a car shot savagely forwards . . .

Maigret almost went into a cafeteria for a bite, but, as he was not far from the St Regis, he suddenly thought of the bar. He was not expecting anything to happen, except perhaps to see MacGill, who'd seemed fond of going there at cocktail time.

And he was there, in fact, with quite a pretty woman. Catching sight of the inspector, he rose halfway in greeting.

Then he must have said something to his companion, because she began staring curiously at Maigret while smoking her lipstick-stained cigarette.

Either MacGill knew nothing or he was remarkably cool-headed, for he seemed very relaxed. As Maigret sat on alone at the bar with his drink, MacGill abruptly decided to excuse himself to his companion and go over to the inspector, holding out his hand.

'I'm rather glad to see you, actually, because after what happened yesterday, I'd intended to speak to you.'

Maigret had pretended not to see the proffered hand, which the secretary finally put in his pocket.

'Little John's behaviour towards you was rude and very clumsy. That's in fact what I wanted to say: he's more tactless than mean-spirited. For a long time he's been used to everyone's complete obedience, and the slightest obstacle or opposition irritates him. And then where his son is concerned, his feelings are very private – if you like, they're the intimate, secret part of his life he keeps jealously to himself. That's why he became angry watching you take an interest in this business despite his objections.

'I can tell you in confidence that ever since your arrival, he's been moving heaven and earth trying to find Jean Maura.

'And he will find him, because he has the means to do so.

'In France, no doubt, where you could be of some help to him, he would accept your assistance. Here, in a city you don't know . . .'

Maigret was absolutely still. He seemed as impassive as a wall.

'So, I do hope that you—'

'Will accept your apologies,' the inspector added calmly.

'. . . And his.'

'Was he the one who told you to offer them to me?'

'What I mean is—'

'That the two of you are anxious, for the same reasons or for different ones, to see me go somewhere else.'

'If you're going to take it like that . . .'

And, turning back to the bar to pick up his glass, a surly Maigret replied, 'I'll take it any way I please.'

When he looked in their direction again, he saw MacGill sitting next to the blonde American, who was asking him questions he obviously had no desire to answer.

The young man looked gloomy, and when the inspector left he felt MacGill gazing after him with both anguish and resentment.

So much the better!

Sent on from the St Regis, a cable awaited him at the Berwick. Ronald Dexter was there as well, waiting patiently for him on a bench in the lobby. The message read:

Received cable excellent news Jean Maura stop will explain situation your return stop investigation pointless now stop expect you next boat stop

Yours sincerely

François d'Hoquélus

Maigret folded the yellow paper into a small rectangle that he slipped inside his wallet with a sigh. Then he turned to the sad clown.

'Have you eaten?'

'Well, I had a hot dog not long ago. But if you want me to keep you company . . .'

And that allowed the inspector to discover another unexpected aspect of his unusual detective. So thin that, even in the smallest sizes, clothes hung loosely on him, Dexter possessed a stomach of outstanding capacity.

Hardly had he sat down at the counter of a cafeteria than his eyes gleamed like those of a man starving for days and he murmured, pointing to some ham-and-cheese sandwiches, 'May I?'

He was asking permission to eat not one sandwich, but the whole stack, and while he proceeded to do so, he kept looking nervously around as if in fear someone would come and put a stop to his meal.

He ate without drinking. Huge mouthfuls disappeared into his astonishingly elastic mouth, and each mouthful pushed the previous one down without causing him the least discomfort.

'I've already found something . . .' he managed nevertheless to say.

And with his free hand, he reached into a pocket of his trenchcoat, which he had not taken the time to remove. He placed a folded paper on the counter. While the inspector unfolded it, he asked, 'Would you mind if I order something hot? It isn't expensive here, you know . . .'

The paper was a handbill of the kind actors once hawked to the audience after their performances.

Get your photos of the artistes here!

And Maigret, who in those days had been a devotee of the Petit Casino at the Porte Saint-Martin, could still hear the eternal refrain.

'Each one costs me ten centimes!'

It wasn't even a postcard like the ones the important acts splurged on, but a simple sheet of poster paper, now a faded yellow.

J and J, the celebrated musical cabaret artistes who have had the honour of playing before all the crowned heads of Europe and the Shah of Persia.

'I must ask you not to get it too dirty,' said the clown as he tackled his bacon and eggs. 'He didn't give it to me, it's only a loan.'

It was laughable, the idea of lending a paper like that when no one would have bothered to pick it up off the street . . .

'He's a friend of mine . . . Well, someone I've known a long time, who used to be a circus ringmaster. It's a lot harder than people think, you know. He was a ringmaster for over forty years, and now he never leaves his armchair, he's very old . . . I went to see him last night because he hardly sleeps at all any more.'

He had his mouth full the whole time he was talking

and was gazing longingly at the sausages someone nearby had just ordered. He would be getting some of those, no question, and probably one of those enormous cakes lacquered with a livid icing that turned Maigret's stomach.

'My friend didn't know J and J personally . . . He was strictly a circus man, you understand? But he has a unique collection of posters, programmes and newspaper articles about circus and vaudeville families. He can tell you that such and such an acrobat, who is now thirty years old, is the son of a particular trapeze artiste who married the granddaughter of the bottom strong man in a pyramid act who got himself killed at the Palladium in London in 1905.'

Maigret listened with one ear and studied the photograph on the slick yellow paper. Could one call it a photograph? The reproduction, a coarse photo-engraving, was so bad that you could hardly distinguish the faces.

Two men, both young, both thin. The biggest difference between them was that one had very long hair. He was the violinist, and Maigret was convinced that he had become Little John.

The other, with sparser hair and, even though young, already going bald, wore glasses; rolling his eyes, he was blowing into a clarinet.

'Of course, go ahead and order some sausages,' Maigret said before Ronald Dexter even opened his mouth.

'You must think I've been hungry all my life, right?'

'Why?'

'Because it's true. I have always been hungry . . . Even when I was earning good money, because I never had enough to eat as much as I'd have liked. You'll have to get that paper back to me because I promised my friend to return it.'

'I'll have it photographed as soon as I can.'

'Oh, I'll have other information, but not right away. Already for that handbill, I had to insist that my friend look for it then and there. He lives in an armchair mounted on wheels, comes and goes in his place cluttered with papers. He assured me that he knew people who could tell us things but he wouldn't say who ... Because he can't remember for sure, I'd bet on that. He needs to rummage around in his clutter.

'He has no telephone. Since he cannot go out, that doesn't help any.

'"Don't worry, people come see me. People come see me," he kept saying. "There are enough artistes who remember old Germain and are happy to come and have a chat in this dump ...

'"I have an old friend who used to be a tightrope walker, then a medium in a spiritualism act and who wound up telling fortunes. She comes every Wednesday.

'"Stop by now and then. When I've got something for you, I'll tell you. But now you must tell me the truth. This is for a book on vaudeville and cabaret acts, isn't it! There's already one on circus folks. For that people used to come here, worm things out of me, carry off my memorabilia and then, when the book came out, my name wasn't even in it ...'"

Maigret could tell what kind of a man Ronald Dexter was and knew that there was no point in rushing him.

'You'll go back there every day . . .'

'I've got other places to visit as well. You'll see, I'll find you all the information you're looking for. Except, I have to ask you for another small advance on expenses. Yesterday you gave me ten dollars, and I've recorded your payment. Look! . . . No, no, I want you to see . . .'

And he showed him a grimy notebook, on one page of which he had written in pencil:

> Received advance for J and J
> investigation: ten dollars.

'Today I'd rather you gave me only five, because I spend everything I get anyway, so it would all go too fast. So then I wouldn't dare ask you for any more, and with no money, I wouldn't be able to help you. It's too much? What about four?'

Maigret took out five dollars and for no reason, when he handed them over, he looked intently at the clown.

Well fed, the man in the trenchcoat wearing an acid green ribbon for a necktie did not look any jollier, but in his eyes there was infinite gratitude, infinite submission mixed with something anxious and trembling. He was like a dog that has finally found a good master and searches humbly for a sign of satisfaction in his face.

It was then that Maigret remembered what O'Brien had said. He remembered old Angelino, too, who that morning had set out on his daily walk and been cruelly killed.

He wondered if he had the right to . . .

But only for a moment: wasn't he sending the former clown into a perfectly quiet part of the city?

'If they ever kill him on me . . .' he thought.

Then he recalled the office in the St Regis, the letter opener that had snapped in the nervous grip of Little John, and MacGill, busy talking about him to his American girl in the bar.

He had never undertaken an investigation in such uncertain and almost crazy circumstances. In reality, no one had instructed him to pursue any investigation. Even old Monsieur d'Hoquélus, so insistent in the house at Meung-sur-Loire, now asked him politely to return to France and mind his own business. Even O'Brien . . .

'I'll drop by to see you tomorrow at around the same time,' said Ronald Dexter, picking up his hat. 'Don't forget that I have to return the handbill.'

J and J . . .

Maigret found himself alone again out on the pavement of an avenue he did not know, and he wandered a good while with his hands in his pockets, his pipe between his teeth, before he glimpsed the lights of a cinema he recognized on Broadway, which set him on the right path.

Suddenly, just like that, he took a notion to write to Madame Maigret and went back to his hotel.

5.

It was between the third and fourth floors that Maigret reflected, without attaching too much importance to it, that he would not want a man such as Special Agent O'Brien, for example, to see what he was up to that morning.

Even people who had worked with him for years and years, like Sergeant Lucas, did not always understand him when he was in this state.

And did he even know himself what he was looking for? For example, at the moment when he stopped for no reason on that step between two floors, staring straight ahead with wide-open but now empty eyes, he must have looked like a man forced by heart trouble to stay stock still wherever he might be and who tries to seem calm to avoid alarming passers-by.

Judging from the number of children younger than seven the inspector was seeing on the stairs, the landings, in the kitchens and bedrooms, the apartment house must have been a swarming mass of kids outside of school hours. Besides, toys lay around in every corner: broken scooters, old soapboxes precariously equipped with wheels, collections of random objects that made no sense for grown-ups yet for their creators must have represented treasures.

There was no concierge, as in French apartment buildings, which complicated Maigret's task. Nothing but numbered, brown-painted letterboxes in the ground-floor corridor, a few with a yellowed visiting card or a name badly engraved on a metal strip.

It was ten in the morning, doubtless the hour when this sort of barracks was most characteristically alive. One out of every two or three doors stood open. Women who hadn't yet combed their hair were doing housework, washing youngsters' faces, shaking none-too-clean carpets out of windows.

'Excuse me, madame . . .'

They looked askance at him. Who could they think he was, this tall man with his heavy overcoat, his hat that he always took off when he spoke to women, whoever they were? Probably someone selling insurance or a new model of electric vacuum cleaner?

And then there was his accent, but it did not stand out here, where there were not only Italians just off the boat, he thought, but Poles and Czechs as well.

'Do you know if there are any tenants left here who moved in about thirty years ago?'

They frowned, because it was just about the last question they expected. In Paris – in Montmartre, for example, or in his old neighbourhood between the République and Bastille Métro stations – there probably wasn't a single decent-sized building where he would not easily have found an elderly man, woman or couple who had lived there for thirty or forty years.

Here they were telling him, 'We moved in only six months ago . . .'

Or a year, or two. At most, four years ago.

83

Without realizing it, instinctively, he would linger at the open doors to observe a Spartan kitchen encumbered by a bed, or a bedroom inhabited by four or five people.

Few tenants knew any others on another floor. Three children, the oldest of whom was a boy of perhaps eight (who doubtless had mumps, given the immense bandage around his head), had begun following him. Then the little boy had grown bolder and was now dashing ahead of Maigret.

'The man wants to know if you were here thirty years ago!'

Still, there were a few elderly people, in armchairs, by the windows, often near a caged canary, the old folks brought over from Europe once a job had been found. And some of them did not understand one word of English.

'I would like to know . . .'

The landings were large and formed a kind of neutral territory where tenants piled up everything not in use in the apartments; on the third-floor landing, a thin woman with blonde hair was doing her wash.

It was here, in one of these honeycomb cells, that J and J had settled in after arriving in New York; here that Little John, now living in a luxurious suite at the St Regis, had spent months, perhaps years.

It would have been hard to concentrate more human lives in so little space, yet that space was without warmth, a place where more than anywhere else one had the feeling of hopeless isolation.

The milk bottles proved it. On the fourth floor,

Maigret stopped short in front of a door, when he saw eight untouched bottles of milk lined up on the straw mat outside it.

He was about to question the boy who had decided to be his benevolent guide when a man of about fifty emerged from the room next door.

'Do you know who lives here?'

The man shrugged without answering, as if to say it was no concern of his.

'You don't know if there's anyone in there?'

'How would you expect me to know?'

'Is it a man, a woman?'

'A man, I think.'

'Old?'

'Depends on what you mean by that. Maybe my age . . . I don't know. He only moved in a month ago.'

Nobody cared what nationality he was or where he came from, and his neighbour, not in the least curious about the bottles of milk, headed down the stairs, only to look back with a frown at this odd visitor asking bizarre questions. Then he went on his way.

Had the tenant of this room gone off on a trip but forgotten to tell the milkman? It was possible. But those who live in such barracks are poor people for whom a penny is a penny. Was he behind that door, perhaps? Living or dead, sick or dying, he could stay there a long time before anyone thought to worry about him.

Even if the tenant had shouted, called for help, would anyone have bothered to check?

A small boy, somewhere, was learning to play the violin.

It was almost excruciating to hear the same phrase clumsily and endlessly repeated, to imagine the awkward bowing unable to draw from the instrument anything but that wretched noise.

Top floor.

'Excuse me, madame: do you know anyone in the house who . . .'

He heard about an old woman whom no one knew, supposedly a long-time tenant there and who had died two months earlier while climbing the stairs with her shopping bag. But she might not have lived there for thirty years . . .

In the end it became annoying to be heralded by this eager kid, who kept scrutinizing him, as if trying to solve the mystery of the stranger who had turned up unexpectedly in his universe.

Enough! Maigret could go back downstairs. He stopped to relight his pipe and continued to sniff the atmosphere around him, imagining a slender, blond young man climbing those same stairs with a violin case under his arm; another young man, with already thinning hair, was playing the clarinet near a window, looking out at the street.

'Hello!'

Maigret scowled instantly. No doubt startled by that reaction, the usually subtly smiling O'Brien – for it was the redhead climbing the stairs to find the inspector – burst into hearty laughter.

The inspector was masking his feelings, in a way, and grumbled awkwardly, 'I thought you weren't having anything to do with this business.'

'Who says I am?'

'Are you going to tell me you've come to visit relatives?'

'First off, that's not in the least impossible, because we all have all kinds of relatives.'

He was in a good mood. Had he figured out what Maigret had been seeking there? He had realized, in any case, that his French colleague was experiencing certain emotions that morning that had touched him in turn, and there was a friendlier look in his eyes than usual.

'I'm not here to have a battle of wits. It's you I'm looking for. Let's go outside, shall we?'

Maigret had already gone down one floor when he changed his mind and went back up a few steps to give a small coin to the little boy, who looked at it without thinking to say thank you.

'Are you beginning to understand New York? I bet you've learned more about it this morning than you would have in a month at the St Regis or the Waldorf.'

They had stopped automatically on the front step, and were both looking at the shop across the street – and at the tailor, old Angelino's son, working at his steam press, because the poor do not have time to dwell on their grief.

A car marked with the police shield was parked a few metres away.

'I dropped by your hotel. When they told me you'd left early, I thought I'd find you here. What I didn't know was that I'd have to plod up to the fifth floor.'

One tiny little jab of irony, an allusion to a certain sensibility – perhaps a certain sentimental streak – that he'd just discovered in this stocky French inspector.

'If you had concierges, as we do, I wouldn't have had to climb all those stairs.'

'You think you wouldn't have done that anyway?'

They got into the car.

'Where are we going?'

'Wherever you want. As of now, it doesn't matter any more. I'll simply drop you off in a more central neighbourhood, less depressing for your mood.'

He lit a pipe. The driver pulled away.

'I have some bad news for you, my dear inspector.'

Why, in that case, was his voice full of sweet satisfaction?

'Jean Maura has been found.'

Maigret turned with a frown and stared at him.

'You don't mean that it's your men who . . .'

'Come, now! Don't be jealous.'

'It isn't jealousy, but . . .'

'But?'

'That wouldn't fit with the rest,' he said more softly, as if to himself. 'No, there's something wrong there.'

'Well, well!'

'What's so surprising?'

'Nothing. Tell me what you think.'

'I don't think. But if Jean Maura has reappeared, if he's alive . . .'

O'Brien nodded in affirmation.

'I wager they simply found him up in the St Regis with his father and MacGill.'

'Bravo, Maigret! That's exactly what happened. In spite of the personal freedom I spoke to you about, perhaps exaggerating a tad to tease you, we do have a few small ways of finding things out, especially in a hotel like the St Regis. Well, this morning, an extra breakfast was ordered for Little John's apartment. Jean Maura was there, settled in the large bedroom adjoining his father's bedroom office.'

'He wasn't questioned?'

'You're forgetting that we have no reason to question him. No law, federal or otherwise, requires passengers disembarking from a ship to dash headlong into their father's arms, and this father never filed a complaint or notified the police of his son's disappearance.'

'One question.'

'If it's a discreet one.'

'Why does Little John – who pays for an elegant suite at the St Regis, as you say, a four- or five-room apartment – personally occupy what we'd call a maid's room and work at a plain pine table, while his secretary sits enthroned behind a fancy mahogany desk?'

'Does it really surprise you?'

'A bit.'

'Here, you see, it doesn't surprise anyone, no more than it does to know that a certain millionaire's son insists on living in the Bronx, which we are now leaving, and on taking the subway every day to his office, when he could easily have at his disposal as many luxury cars as he wanted.

'That detail you mentioned about Little John is well known. It's part of his legend. Every successful man has a legend, and his works very well; the popular press publications refer to it often.

'The man who has become rich and powerful recreates, at the St Regis, the room of his youthful beginnings and lives there simply, disdaining the luxury of the other rooms.

'As for knowing whether Little John is sincere or managing his public relations, that is a different question.'

For some reason Maigret found himself responding without hesitation, 'He is sincere.'

'Ah!'

Then they were silent for a while.

'Perhaps you would like to learn the pedigree of MacGill, of whom you do not seem inordinately fond? I just happen to have been told these things, remember, this is not police information.'

Even though O'Brien was only joking, Maigret found this constant doublespeak exasperating.

'I'm listening.'

'He was born in New York twenty-eight years ago, probably in the Bronx, of unknown parentage. For a few months, I'm not sure exactly how many, he was cared for by a children's aid society in a suburb of the city.

'He was removed by a man who stated that he wished to take responsibility for him and who provided the requisite moral and financial guarantees for such cases.'

'Little John . . .'

'Who was not yet called Little John and who had recently established a small business in second-hand phonographs. The child was entrusted to a certain Mrs MacGill, a Scotswoman, the widow of a funeral-home employee. The woman and child left the country to go and live in Canada, in St Jerome. As a young man, MacGill studied in nearby Montreal, which explains why he speaks French as well as he does English. Then, when he was around twenty, he disappeared from circulation to resurface six months ago as Little John's private secretary. That's all I know and I can't guarantee that this hearsay is accurate.

'And now, what will you do?'

He displayed his mellowest, most aggravating smile with his least expressive countenance.

'Are you going to visit your client? After all, young Maura is the one who turned to you and who—'

'I don't know.'

Maigret was furious. Because it really was no longer Jean Maura and his fears that interested him but his father, Little John, and the house at 169th Street, and a certain cabaret handbill, and finally an old Italian named Angelino Giacomi someone had run over like a dog while he was crossing the street.

He would go to the St Regis, obviously, because he could not do otherwise. They would undoubtedly tell him again that they had no need of him and would offer him a cheque and passage on a ship to France.

His wisest course would be to go home the way he had come, even if it meant spending the rest of his days being wary of all the young men and Messrs d'Hoquélus in creation.

'Shall I drop you off there?'

'Where?'

'At the St Regis.'

'If you want.'

'Shall I see you this evening? I think I will be free for dinner. If you are as well, call me, I'll come and pick you up at your hotel or elsewhere. Today is a lucky day: I've the use of an official car. I wonder if we'll be drinking to your departure?'

And his eyes said no. He had understood Maigret so well! But he needed to shrug off the slightest emotion with a pleasantry.

'Good luck!'

What lay ahead was the worst part, a thankless task. Maigret could have predicted almost exactly what would happen: nothing surprising, nothing of interest, but he felt obliged to go through with it.

He went up to the reception desk, as he had when first arriving.

'Would you please announce me to Mr Jean Maura?'

The clerk had been briefed, for he promptly picked up the phone.

'Mr MacGill? There is someone here asking for Mr Jean Maura . . . I believe so, yes. Let me make sure . . . And you are, sir?'

The inspector told him his name.

'That's right,' confirmed the clerk. 'Of course. I will send him up.'

So MacGill had known from the first moment who was at the desk.

A bellboy took him upstairs once more. He recognized the floor, the corridor, the apartment.

'Come in!'

And a smiling MacGill came towards him, seemingly

without the least resentment and, as if relieved of a great weight, holding out his hand without appearing to remember that Maigret had ignored it the day before.

When he did again, MacGill exclaimed evenly, 'Still put out, my dear inspector?'

Hmm! He had always said simply 'inspector' before, and this familiar touch was perhaps not insignificant.

'You see, we were right, the boss and I, and you were wrong. Speaking of which! I must first congratulate you regarding your police connection: you were quick to hear about the prodigal son's return.'

He went and opened the door to the next room. Jean Maura was there with his father and, the first to notice the inspector, he blushed.

'Your friend Maigret,' announced MacGill, 'would like to speak to you. If you don't mind, sir?'

Little John stepped into the office as well, but merely nodded absently at the inspector. As for the young man, he came over and shook his hand, appearing embarrassed and ill at ease.

He turned his head away and mumbled, 'I must apologize.'

MacGill still seemed brimming with carefree good humour, whereas Little John, on the contrary, looked tired and careworn. He probably hadn't slept the night before. His gaze, for the first time, was evasive, and to bolster his confidence he felt the need to light one of those fat cigars made especially for him with his initials on the band.

His hand shook a little as he struck the match. He, too,

must have been in a hurry to get this unavoidable farce over with.

'What are you apologizing for?' asked Maigret, well aware that this was expected of him.

'Of having gone off and left you so rudely. You see, I spotted a fellow I'd known last year among the journalists who came on board; he had a pocket flask of whisky and absolutely insisted on celebrating my arrival . . .'

Maigret did not inquire where this scene had occurred on the ship because he knew it was purely imaginary, concocted for the young man by MacGill or Little John.

By the former, probably, who assumed too detached and indifferent an air during his pupil's recitation, like a teacher who won't prompt his favourite.

'He had some girls with him in the taxi.'

How plausible was that, this newsman going off to work at ten in the morning taking women along! They weren't bothering to make it believable. They were tossing him any old explanation to chew on, without caring to see if he would believe it or not. Why bother? Wasn't he now out of the game?

Curiously enough, Jean Maura was much less fatigued than his father. He had the look of a young man who has slept soundly and he seemed more embarrassed than worried.

'I should have let you know. I did look for you out on deck.'

'No!'

Why had Maigret said that?

'That's true, I didn't look for you. I'd been on my best

behaviour too long while we crossed. I didn't dare drink in front of you except that last night. You remember? And I didn't even apologize to you right away.'

As on the previous day, Little John had gone to stand by the window, holding back the curtain with what must have been a familiar gesture.

As for MacGill, he made a point of bustling around like a man only half-listening to the conversation, even going so far as to make a routine telephone call.

'Care for a cocktail, inspector?'

'No, thank you.'

'As you wish.'

Jean Maura was winding things up.

'I don't know what happened next. That's the first time I was ever completely drunk. We went to lots of places, we were drinking with lots of people I wouldn't recognize if I ever saw them again.'

'At the Donkey Bar?' asked Maigret, with a cynical glance at MacGill.

'I don't know . . . it's possible . . . There was a party given by some people my friend knows . . .'

'In the country?'

This time Jean Maura shot a quick look at MacGill, who had his back turned, however, so the young man had to answer on his own.

'Yes . . . In the country . . . We drove there.'

'And you returned only last evening?'

'Yes.'

'They brought you back?'

'Yes. No . . . I mean, they drove me back to the city.'

'But not to the hotel?'

Another glance at MacGill.

'No . . . not to the hotel . . . I'm the one who didn't want that, because I was ashamed.'

'I assume you do not need me any more?'

This time he looked at his father as if to appeal for help, and it was puzzling to see Little John, the man of action par excellence, remaining aloof from the conversation as if it did not concern him. And yet it did concern his son, to whom he wrote so tenderly that he might almost have been composing love letters . . .

'I had a long conversation with my father.'

'And with Mr MacGill?'

He did not answer yes, or no. He almost denied it, then caught himself and went on.

'I feel bad about having made you come so far on account of my childish fears. I know how worried you've been . . . I wonder if you will ever forgive me for having left you completely at a loss about my whereabouts.'

As he spoke, he, too, seemed to grow astonished at his father's attitude, and looked imploringly at him for rescue.

And it was MacGill, yet again, who took the situation in hand.

'Don't you think, sir, that it might be time to conclude any unfinished business with the inspector?'

Then Little John turned around, tapped the ash off his cigar with his little finger, walked over to the mahogany desk.

'I believe,' he said, 'that there is not much business to conclude. I apologize, inspector, for not having received you with all due cordiality. I thank you for having looked after my son with such solicitude. I will ask you simply to accept the cheque that my secretary will give you and which is but slight compensation for the trouble we have caused you, my son and I.'

He hesitated an instant, doubtless wondering whether he would shake hands with the inspector; in the end he bowed slightly, somewhat abruptly, and walked towards the connecting door, signalling Jean to follow him.

'Goodbye, inspector,' said the young man, quickly shaking Maigret's hand.

He added, with what seemed complete sincerity, 'I'm not afraid any more, you know.'

He smiled. A smile still a touch pale, like the smile of a convalescent. Then he disappeared after his father into the next room.

The cheque was already filled out in the chequebook lying on the desk. Without sitting down, MacGill detached it and handed it to Maigret, expecting, perhaps, that he would refuse it.

Instead, Maigret looked calmly at the amount: two thousand dollars. Then he carefully folded the slip of paper and placed it inside his wallet, saying, 'Thank you.'

That was all. The oppressive scene was over. He was leaving. He had not said goodbye to MacGill, who had followed him to the door and finally closed it behind him.

Despite his horror of cocktails and foolishly luxurious places, Maigret stopped at the bar and tossed down two Manhattans, one after the other.

Then he headed on foot towards his hotel and as he

walked he nodded his head from time to time, moving his lips like someone having a long discussion with himself.

Hadn't the clown promised him to be at the Berwick at the same time as before?

He was there, on the sofa, but his eyes were so sad and his expression so anguished that it was clear he'd been drinking.

'I know you're going to call me a weak coward,' he began, standing up. 'And it's true, you see, that I'm a coward. I knew what would happen and I still couldn't resist.'

'Have you had lunch?'

'Not yet . . . But I'm not hungry. No, strange as that may seem, I'm not hungry, because I'm too ashamed of myself. I'd have done better not to let you see me like this. And yet I only had two little drinks. Gin . . . Mind you, I chose gin because it's the weakest spirit. Otherwise, I would have drunk scotch. I was very tired and told myself, "Ronald, if you have a gin, just one . . ."

'Only, I had three . . . Did I say three? . . . I don't know any more . . . I'm disgusting, and I did this with your money.

'Throw me out on my ear. . .

'Wait, no, don't do that yet, because I have something for you . . . Hang on . . . Something important, it will come back to me . . . If we were out in the fresh air, at least . . . How about going outside for some air?'

He sniffled, blew his nose.

'I wouldn't mind a bite, after all . . . Not before I've told you . . . One moment – yes – I saw my friend again, yesterday evening . . . Germain. You remember Germain? Poor Germain! Imagine a man who's had an active life, who has followed circuses around the entire world and who's nailed to a wheelchair.

'Admit it, he'd be better off dead . . . What am I saying? Never think that I wish him dead. But if I were the one it was going to happen to, I would rather be dead. That's what I meant.

'Well . . . I was right to claim that Germain would do anything for me . . . He's a man who would give his right arm for others.

'He doesn't look like much. He's grumpy. You'd think he was a selfish old man. And yet, he spent hours going through his files, looking for traces of J and J. Look, I've got another paper.'

He blanched, turned green, searched through his pockets in anguish and seemed almost about to burst into tears.

'I deserve to be . . .'

Well, no. He deserved nothing, because he had finally found the document, beneath his handkerchief.

'It isn't very clean. But you'll understand.'

This time it was the programme for a road company that had toured the American hinterland thirty years earlier. In big letters, the name of a chanteuse whose photograph graced the cover; then other names: a couple of tightrope walkers, a comic named Robson, Lucille the Seer and at last, at the very bottom of the list, the musical cabaret artistes J and J.

'Take a good look at those names. Robson died in a train accident ten or fifteen years ago, I forget . . . Germain was the one who told me. You remember I mentioned yesterday that Germain had an elderly lady friend who came to see him every Wednesday? Don't you find that touching, hmm? . . . And you know, there was never anything between the two of them, not a thing!'

He was getting teary again.

'I've never seen her. It seems she was very thin and pale in those days, so pale that they called her the Angel. Well! Now she's so fat that . . . We are going to eat, aren't we? I don't know if it's the gin, but I've got cramps . . . It's disgusting to ask you for more money . . . What was I saying? The Angel, Lucile . . . Germain's old friend . . . Today's Wednesday. She ought to be at his place at around five o'clock. She'll bring a little cake, as she does every week . . . I swear to you that if we go, I won't touch it . . . because this old woman they called the Angel and who brings a cake every week to Germain . . .'

'Have you told your friend we were coming?'

'I told him we might . . . I could come by for you at half past four . . . It's quite far, especially on the subway, because he's not on a direct line.'

'Let's go!'

Maigret had abruptly resolved not to let his definitely too-gloomy clown out of his sight and, after he made him eat something, he took him back to his hotel and put him to bed on the green plush couch.

After that, as he had the previous evening, he wrote a long letter to Madame Maigret.

6.

Maigret followed his clown up the creaking staircase and because Dexter, God knows why, felt he ought to walk on his tiptoes, the inspector found himself doing so too.

The sad man had slept off his gin, however, and although his eyes were still puffy and his speech a touch thick, he had abandoned his tone of lamentation for a somewhat firmer voice.

He'd been the one to give the cabbie an address in Greenwich Village, and Maigret was discovering, in the heart of New York, a few minutes from its big modern buildings, a tiny city within the city, almost a provincial town, with its houses no taller than in Bordeaux or Dijon, its shops, its quiet streets where people could stroll, its inhabitants who seemed not to notice the monstrous city all around them.

'We're here,' Dexter had announced.

Sensing something like fear in the voice of this man in his grimy raincoat, Maigret had looked his companion straight in the face.

'Are you sure you told him I was coming?'

'I said that you might come.'

'And what did you tell him I was?'

He had expected this. The clown became troubled.

'I was going to speak to you about that . . . I didn't know

how to deal with the matter because Germain, you see, has become quite unsociable. What's more, when I came to see him that first time, he made me have a quick little drink or two. I don't precisely recall what I told him . . . That you were a very rich man, that you were looking for a son you'd never seen . . . You mustn't be mad at me, it was all for the best . . . He was moved, in the end, and I'm sure that's why he started combing his files right away.'

It was ridiculous. The inspector thought about what the clown could have concocted with a few drinks under his belt.

And now Dexter was becoming increasingly hesitant the closer they came to the former ringmaster's door. Might he not have lied all up and down the line, even to Maigret? No, after all: there was the photograph, and the handbill . . .

Light under a door. A faint murmuring. Dexter stammering, 'Knock . . . There's no doorbell.'

Maigret knocked. Silence fell. Someone coughed. The sound of a cup set down on a saucer.

'Come in!'

And they felt as if simply crossing the narrow barrier of a dilapidated doormat had taken them on an immense voyage through time and space. They were no longer in New York, next door to skyscrapers that at this hour were darting all their lights up into the Manhattan sky. Was it even still the age of electricity?

Anyone in the room would have sworn it was lit by a paraffin lamp, an impression created by the large shade of pleated red silk on a floor lamp.

There was but a single circle of light in the centre of the room and within it a man in a wheelchair, an old man who must once have been quite stout and was still bulky enough to completely fill the chair, but who was now so flaccid that he seemed to have suddenly deflated. A few white hairs of impressive length floated around his naked pate as he craned his head forwards to see the intruders over the rims of his glasses.

'Excuse me for disturbing you,' Maigret began, while the clown hid behind him.

There was someone else in the room, as fat as Germain, with a mauve complexion, unnaturally blonde hair and a small, smiling, lipstick-smeared mouth.

Hadn't they stumbled into some corner of a wax museum? No, for the figures were moving, and tea was steaming in the two cups sitting on a side table next to a sliced cake.

'Ronald Dexter told me that tonight I might perhaps find here the information I'm looking for.'

You couldn't see the walls, they were so plastered with posters and photographs. A lungeing whip, its shaft still wound with colourful ribbons, was in a place of honour.

'Would you provide chairs for these gentlemen, Lucile?'

The voice had remained what it doubtless was in the days when the man announced the entrance of the clowns and tumblers into the ring, and it resounded strangely in this too-small room so cluttered that poor Lucile found it hard to clear off two black chairs with red velvet seats.

'This young man who knew me long ago . . .' the old man was saying.

Was this phrase not a poem in itself? First, Dexter became a young man in the old ringmaster's eyes. Then there was the 'who knew me long ago' instead of 'whom I knew long ago'.

'. . . has informed me of your distressing predicament. If your son had belonged to the circus world, if only for a few weeks, I can assure you that you would have had only to come and tell me, "Germain, it was in such-and-such a year that he appeared in such-and-such an act . . . He was like this and like that . . ." and Germain would not have had to search through his archives.'

He gestured towards the piles of papers everywhere, on the furniture, the floor, even on the bed, for Lucile had had to place some there to clear the two chairs.

'Germain had all that here.'

He pointed to his skull and tapped it with that finger.

'But where vaudeville and cabarets are concerned, I say this to you: you must consult my old friend Lucile. She is here . . . Listening to you . . . Speak, then, to her.'

Maigret had let his pipe go out and yet he needed it to regain a foothold in reality. Holding the pipe in his hand, he must have looked embarrassed, for the fat lady spoke to him with a fresh smile that resembled, thanks to her innocently garish make-up, that of a doll.

'You may smoke . . . Robson smoked a pipe, too. I smoked one myself, during the years right after his death . . . Perhaps you wouldn't understand, but it was still a bit of his presence.'

'Your act was a very interesting one,' murmured the inspector politely.

'The best of its kind, I can only agree. Everyone will tell you: Robson was unique . . . His imposing presence, above all, and you cannot imagine how much that counts in our kind of number. He wore a frock coat, waistcoat, tight breeches with stockings of black silk. His calves were magnificent . . .

'Wait!'

She searched, not through a handbag, but in a silk reticule with a silver clasp, and pulled out a publicity photograph of her husband attired as she had described, with a black velvet mask over his eyes, a waxed moustache, 'making a leg' and brandishing a magician's wand at his invisible audience.

'And here I am at that same time.'

An ageless woman, slender, sad, diaphanous, with her hands crossed under her chin in the most artificial pose imaginable, staring vacantly into the distance.

'I can say that we toured throughout the world. In certain countries Robson wore a red silk cape over his outfit and in a red spotlight he looked truly diabolical in the magic coffin number . . . I trust you believe in mental telepathy?'

The room was stifling. Although Maigret was desperate for a rush of fresh air, thick drapes of faded plush masked the windows, as heavy as an old stage curtain. Who knows? He had the feeling they had perhaps been cut out of that very thing.

'Germain told me that you were looking for your son or your brother.'

'My brother,' replied the inspector hastily, suddenly

realizing that neither of the J and J artistes could plausibly be his son.

'That's what I thought . . . I hadn't completely understood . . . That's why I expected to see an older man. Which of the two was your brother? The violin or the clarinet?'

'I do not know, madame.'

'What do you mean, you don't know?'

'My brother disappeared when he was a baby. It's only recently, by chance, that we've picked up his trail again.'

This was ludicrous. This was unbearable. And yet, it was impossible to tell the simple truth to these two, who revelled in fantasy. Forbearance was almost Christian charity towards them, and the cream of the jest was, that imbecile Dexter, despite knowing the truth, seemed to believe the make-believe and was already beginning to sniffle.

'Step into the light, so I can see your face . . .'

'I do not believe there was any resemblance between my brother and me.'

'How do you know, when he was kidnapped so young . . .'

Kidnapped! Honestly! Now they had to play this farce out to the very end.

'In my opinion, it must have been Joachim . . . No, wait: there's a suggestion of Joseph in the forehead . . . But . . . Haven't I got their names mixed up, in fact? Just imagine, I used to do that all the time . . . There was one with long blond hair like a girl, about the same colour as mine . . .'

'Joachim, I think,' said Maigret.

'Let me remember . . . How would you know? . . . The

other one had slightly broader shoulders and wore glasses. It's funny. We all lived together for almost a year, and there are things I can't recall, others that come back to me as if it were yesterday . . . We'd all signed on for a tour through the Southern states: Mississippi, Louisiana, Texas. It was very hard, because the people down there were still practically savages. Some of them rode to the show on horses. Once, they killed a Negro during our number, I don't remember why any more.

'What I'm wondering is, which one of the two was Jessie with.

'Was it Jessie or Bessie? . . . Bessie, I think . . . No, Jessie! I'm sure it was Jessie, because I mentioned one time that it made three Js: Joseph, Joachim and Jessie.'

If only Maigret had been able to ask questions, calmly, to elicit precise answers! But he had to let her ramble through the complicated meanderings of her thoughts, an old woman who had probably always been a trifle scatterbrained.

'Poor little Jessie. She was touching. I'd taken her under my protection, because she was in a delicate situation.'

What could that delicate situation have been? This would probably become clear in time.

'She was small and slender. I was small and slender, too, in those days, fragile as a flower. They called me the Angel, did you know?'

'I know.'

'It was Robson who gave me that name. He didn't say "my angel", which is banal, but "the Angel" – I don't know whether you see the nuance . . . Bessie – no, Jessie – was quite young. I wonder if she was even eighteen. And you could sense that she'd been unhappy. I never learned where they'd found her . . . I say "they" because I don't remember whether it was Joseph or Joachim. Since those three were always together, naturally you wondered.'

'What was her role in your tour?'

'She didn't have one. She was not a performer. She was an orphan, surely, because I never saw her write to anyone. They must have plucked her from beside her mother's deathbed.'

'And she followed the company?'

'She followed us everywhere. A hard life. The manager was a brute. Did you know him, Germain?'

'His brother is still in New York. I heard some talk about him last week. He sells programmes at Madison Square Garden.'

'He used to treat us like dogs. Robson was the only one who stood up to him . . . I think that if he could have got away with it, he'd have fed us like beasts on animal mash to economize on food. We stayed in dirty holes full of bedbugs . . . He wound up abandoning us fifty miles from New Orleans, ran off with the cashbox, and once again it was Robson . . .'

Fortunately, she suddenly decided to nibble a piece of cake. That provided a brief respite, but she swiftly continued, wiping her lips with a lace hankie.

'J and J, pardon me for telling you so, since one of the two is your brother (I bet that it's Joseph), but J and J were not artistes like us, with star billing, they came at the tail end of the programme. There's no dishonour in that . . . Please don't be angry at me if I've hurt your feelings!'

'No, no, of course not!'

'They earned very little, nothing, so to speak, but their travel expenses were paid, and the food, if you could call it that. Only, there was Jessie . . . They had to pay for Jessie's train tickets. And the meals. Not always for the meals . . . Hold on, it's coming back to me . . . I believe I am in contact with Robson.'

And her enormous bosom swelled within her bodice as she wiggled her chubby little fingers.

'Forgive me, sir . . . I assume that you believe in the afterlife? If not, you would not be so passionately searching for your brother, who may well be dead. I sense that Robson has just entered into communication with me . . . I know it, I'm sure of it. Allow me to turn my thoughts to him, and he will tell me himself all that you need to know.'

The clown was so awed that he gave a kind of moan. Or perhaps it was because of the cake, which no one had thought to offer him?

Maigret stared intently at the floor, wondering how much longer he could bear this.

'Yes, Robson, I'm listening . . . Germain, would you dim the light?'

They must both have been used to these spiritualist séances, for without leaving his wheelchair, Germain reached out to the lamp and pulled a little chain, turning off one of the light bulbs under the red silk shade.

'I see them, yes . . . Near a wide river . . . And there are cotton plantations everywhere . . . Help me some more,

109

Robson dear. Help me the way you used to do . . . A big table . . . We're all there and you're in the place of honour . . . J and J. Wait. She is between the two of us. A fat Negro woman is serving us . . .'

The clown moaned again, but she continued in the monotone she must have used long ago in her performance as a medium.

'Jessie is very pale . . . We've been on the train . . . Travelling for a long time . . . The train has stopped in the middle of the countryside . . . Everyone is exhausted . . . The manager has gone out to put up the posters . . . And J and J are each cutting off a piece of their meat to give to Jessie.'

It would have been simpler for her, obviously, to relate these things without the mystico-theatrical rubbish. Maigret felt like telling her, 'Facts, please? And talk like a normal person.'

But if someone like Lucile had begun to talk like a normal person, and Germain to see his memorabilia for what it was, would either of them have had the strength to go on living?

'And wherever I see them it's the same . . . Those two are by her side, sharing their meals . . . Because they haven't enough money to buy her a real dinner.'

'You said that the tour lasted a year?'

She pretended to struggle, opened fluttering eyelids, stammered, 'Did I say something? . . . Please forgive me . . . I was with Robson . . .'

'I was asking you how long the tour lasted.'

'More than a year. We'd set out for three or four months. But lots of unexpected things happen on the road, it's always that way. Then there's the question of money. There's never enough money to come home. So the tour goes on, from town to town and even to villages.'

'Do you know which one of the men was in love with Jessie?'

'I don't. Perhaps it was Joachim? He was your brother, right? . . . I'm convinced you look somewhat like Joachim. He was my favourite and played the violin magnificently. Not in his act, because there he only did improvisations. But when we happened to stay for a day or two in the same hotel . . .'

He could see her, in some plain board hotel in Texas or Louisiana, darning her husband's black silk stockings . . . And this Jessie who at meals nibbled humbly on a little of the two men's share.

'You never knew what became of them?'

'As I told you, the troupe fell apart in New Orleans when the manager left us stranded. Robson and I got an engagement right away, because our act was well known. I don't know how the others earned the money for the train.'

'You returned immediately to New York?'

'I believe so. I no longer remember exactly. I do know that I saw one of the two Js again in the office of a Broadway impresario; that must not have been too long afterwards. What makes me think so is that I'd put on one of the dresses I'd worn during the tour . . . Which of the two men was it? . . . It struck me that I was seeing him on his own. We never saw one without the other . . .'

Abruptly, when no one expected it, Maigret shot to his

feet. He felt he could not last five minutes more in that stifling atmosphere.

'Please forgive my intrusion here,' he said, turning to Germain.

'If it had been a question of the circus instead of the vaudeville circuit,' repeated the former ringmaster, like an old record.

And she: 'I'll give you my address. I still give private consultations. I have a small clientele of very nice people, who trust me. And I can tell the truth to you: it's Robson who continues to help me. I don't always admit this, because some people are afraid of spirits.'

She handed him a card that he shoved into his pocket. The clown gazed one last time at the cake and grabbed his hat.

'I thank you again.'

Oof! He had never gone down any stairs faster and, once out in the street, he breathed in great gasps: he felt as if he were setting foot once more on solid ground, and the street lamps suddenly looked like friends one sees again after a long absence.

There were bright shops, passers-by, a boy of flesh and blood hopping along at the edge of the pavement.

True, the clown was still there, who managed to murmur dolefully, 'I did what I could . . .'

Another five dollars, naturally!

They were dining together again in a French restaurant. Back at the Berwick, Maigret had found a phone message from O'Brien, asking him to call as soon as he returned.

'As hoped, I'm free this evening,' the agent announced shortly afterwards. 'If you are, too, we could have dinner and a talk.'

They had already been sitting across from each other for more than fifteen minutes, and O'Brien had yet to say anything to the inspector; while ordering his meal, he had merely sent a few ironic and complacent little smiles his way.

'Did you not notice,' he finally murmured, slicing into a magnificent châteaubriand, 'that you were being followed again?'

The inspector frowned, not because he felt immediately alarmed, but from vexation at not having been more careful.

'I noticed right away, picking you up at the Berwick. It isn't Bill this time, but someone who ran over old Angelino. I bet anything you like he's just outside.'

'We'll certainly see when we leave.'

'I don't know when he went on duty . . . Did you leave the hotel earlier this afternoon?'

And this time, Maigret looked up with anguished eyes, thought for a moment and slammed his fist on the table with a 'Shit!' that made his companion grin.

'Have you been up to something really compromising?'

'Your man's dark, obviously, since he's Sicilian . . . Wears a very light grey hat, does he?'

'Exactly.'

'In that case, he was in the hotel lobby when I came down from my room with my clown, towards five o'clock. We bumped into each other while both making for the door.'

'So, he's been following you since five.'

'And therefore . . .'

Was it going to be like it had been with poor Angelino all over again?

'Can't you people in the FBI do something to protect people?' he asked irritably.

'That might depend on the danger threatening them.'

'Would you have protected the old tailor?'

'Knowing what I do now, yes.'

'Then there are two other people to protect, and I think you'd do well to take all necessary steps before finishing that châteaubriand.'

He gave him Germain's address. Then he held out the clairvoyant's card he had had in his pocket.

'There should be a telephone here.'

'Pardon me . . .'

Well, well . . . The unflappable and blandly smiling O'Brien was no longer waxing ironic or championing that famous personal freedom!

Since the agent was on the telephone for a long time, Maigret went to glance out at the street. On the pavement across the way, he recognized the pale grey hat he had seen in his hotel lobby and when he sat down again he swiftly dispatched two large glasses of wine.

O'Brien returned soon after and was polite – or perhaps wicked – enough not to ask a single question and quietly picked up his meal where he had left off.

'In short,' grumbled Maigret, eating without any appetite, 'if I had not gone there, old Angelino would probably not be dead.'

He was waiting for denials, hoping for them, but O'Brien simply said, 'Probably.'

'In that case, if there are other accidents . . .'

'They will be your fault, won't they . . . Is that what you think? It's what I think, and have thought, from the very first day. Do you remember when we had dinner together that evening you arrived?'

'Does this mean that those people must be left alone?'

'It's too late, now.'

'What do you mean?'

'It's too late, because we're looking into it too, because even if you give up the chase, if you sail tomorrow to Le Havre or Cherbourg, they will continue to feel hunted.'

'Little John?'

'I've no idea.'

'MacGill?'

'I don't know. I'll say at once that I'm not the one in charge of this case. Tomorrow or the next day, when the time is right, when my colleague tells me – because he's conducting the investigation, which is none of my business – I will introduce you to him. He's a good man.'

'Along your lines?'

'The complete opposite. That's why I say he's a good man. I just phoned him . . . He would appreciate my giving him a few details soon about these two people he's to protect.'

'It's an insane story!' groaned Maigret.

'What?'

'I'm telling you, it's an insane story! Because they are – if not authentic lunatics – two poor maniacs at the very least, who risk paying with their lives for the indiscretions they committed on my behalf . . . And not only that: without meaning to, because of that crying-clown imbecile, I played on their sympathies to win them over.'

O'Brien watched wide-eyed as a nervous Maigret snapped out his words while he chewed his food in a sort of rage.

'No doubt you'll tell me that what I learned isn't much and that the game wasn't worth the candle. It's possible, however, that we do not have precisely the same ideas about police investigations.'

His companion's cloying smile was driving him crazy.

'My visit this morning to the house on 169th Street amused you as well, didn't it, and you would doubtless have had a good laugh if you'd seen me, preceded by a little boy, sniffing around and poking my nose in everywhere.

'Nevertheless, in spite of arriving in America just a few days ago, I claim to now know more than you do about Little John and the other J.

'A question of temperament, probably. You need facts, don't you, definite facts, while I . . .'

Seeing O'Brien about to burst out laughing, despite struggling mightily not to, Maigret stopped abruptly and decided to laugh as well.

'Please forgive me . . . I just went through the most idiotic moments of my life . . . Listen to this . . .'

He recounted his visit to old Germain, described Lucile in her trances (or fake ones) and concluded by asking, 'Now do you understand why I'm afraid for them? Angelino knew something, and they didn't hesitate to remove him. Did Angelino know more than the others? It's likely. But I stayed a whole hour in the former ringmaster's place. Lucile was there.'

'That's true. Still, I don't think the danger is as serious.'

'Because you think as I do, I bet, that 169th Street is where those people feel at risk?'

O'Brien nodded.

'What we really need to know is whether this Jessie also lived in the building across from the tailor shop. Is it possible to search the police archives for traces of any serious incident or accident that might have occurred in that house thirty years ago?'

'It's more complicated than in your country. Especially if the event in question was not what I might call official, if there was no investigation . . . In France, I remember, there would be a record at police headquarters of every tenant who had lived in a house and, if appropriate, mention of their deaths.'

'Because you also believe . . .'

'I don't believe anything. I repeat, this is not my investigation. I'm on a completely different case and will be for weeks, if not months. Later, after we've had our brandy, I'll call my colleague. A propos, I know that he went to the Immigration Bureau this afternoon. There, at least, they keep a record of everyone who enters the United States. Wait . . . I wrote something down on a piece of paper . . .'

Always the same nonchalance, as if to downplay the importance of what he was doing. Perhaps, in the end, it was more a kind of reticence vis-à-vis Maigret than any administrative precaution?

'Here's the date of Maura's entry into the United States: "Joachim-Jean-Marie Maura, born in Bayonne, age twenty-two, violinist". The name of the ship, long gone: "the *Aquitaine*". As for the other J, he could only be "Joseph-Ernest-Dominique Daumale, age twenty-four, born in Bayonne" as well. He's not listed as a clarinettist, but as a composer. I believe you see the difference?

'I was given one more piece of information, which is perhaps of no importance, but which I feel you should have. Two and a half years after his arrival here, Joachim Maura, already calling himself John Maura, and who gave as his address the building that you know at 169th Street, left America for Europe, where he remained just short of ten months.

'After which time we note his return aboard an English vessel, the *Mooltan*.

'I do not believe my colleague is bothering to cable France regarding this matter. But, knowing you . . .'

Maigret had thought of that precisely when O'Brien had mentioned Bayonne. Already, in his mind, he was writing the cable for the police of that city.

Urgent request all details Joachim-Jean-Marie Maura and Joseph-Ernest-Dominique Daumale, left France . . .

It was the American's idea to order two old Armagnacs in snifters. He was also the first to light his pipe.

'What are you thinking about?' he asked, as Maigret

sat impassive and thoughtful, his snifter cupped under his nose.

'Jessie.'

'And you're wondering? . . .'

It was almost a game they were playing, the one man with his everlasting yet discreetly faint smile, the other with his frowning pretence of ill humour.

'I'm wondering whose mother she is!'

For an instant, the redhead's smile faded as he sipped and murmured, 'That will depend on the death certificate, won't it?'

They had understood each other. Neither one felt like voicing his thoughts any further.

Maigret, however, could not help grumbling, feigning a bad mood that had already passed.

'If we find it! What with your damned personal freedom that prevents you from keeping a record of who lives and who dies!'

In reply, O'Brien simply pointed to their empty glasses and called, 'Waiter, the same again!'

And added, 'Your poor Sicilian must be dying of thirst out on the sidewalk.'

7.

It was late, probably close to ten o'clock. Maigret's watch had stopped and unlike the St Regis, the Berwick did not spoil its guests by setting electric clocks in its walls. Anyway, why bother knowing the time? Maigret was in no hurry that morning. Actually, he had no plans at all. For the first time since he had landed in New York, he was greeted when he awakened by real springtime sunshine, a tiny bit of which had filtered in to his room and bathroom.

Because of this sun, moreover, he had hung his shaving mirror from the window latch and was shaving there, as he used to do in Paris at Boulevard Richard-Lenoir, where there was always a ray of sunlight on his cheek when he shaved in the morning. Isn't it wrong to believe that big cities are all different from one another, even in the case of New York, which is always written about as a kind of monstrous machine that grinds people to pieces?

He, Maigret, was there, in New York, and he had a window latch at just the right height for shaving, a slanting ray of sunshine to make him blink and, across the way in some office or studio building, two girls in white smocks laughing at him.

That morning, as it happened, he wound up shaving in three stages, because he was interrupted twice by the phone ringing. The first time, the voice sounded far way, of recent memory yet unrecognizable.

'Hello . . . Inspector Maigret?'

'Yes.'

'You're really Inspector Maigret?'

'Yes, I am.'

'It's Inspector Maigret on the phone?'

'Yes, dammit!'

Then the voice shifted from mournful to tragic.

'Ronald Dexter here.'

'Yes. And?'

'I'm so sorry to disturb you, but I absolutely must see you.'

'You have some news?'

'I beg you to see me as soon as possible.'

'Are you far from here?'

'Not very.'

'It's urgent?'

'Quite urgent.'

'In that case, come right away to my room at the hotel.'

'Thank you.'

Maigret had smiled at first. Then, upon reflection, he remembered something in the clown's tone that worried him.

Barely had he returned to lathering his cheeks when the telephone summoned him back into the bedroom, where he hastily wiped his face clean.

'Hello.'

'Inspector Maigret?'

A crisp voice, this time, almost excessively so; French with a pronounced American accent.

'Speaking.'

'Lieutenant Lewis here!'

'I'm listening . . .'

'My colleague O'Brien informed me that I should get in touch with you as soon as possible. Might we perhaps meet this morning?'

'Forgive me, lieutenant, for asking you this, but my watch has stopped. What time is it?'

'Ten thirty.'

'I would have been glad to come to your office. Unfortunately, a moment ago I agreed to see someone in my hotel room. And it's possible, even probable, that the meeting will concern something of interest to you. Would you mind coming to see me in my room at the Berwick?'

'I'll be there in twenty minutes.'

'Has there been some new development?'

Maigret was sure that the lieutenant had still been on the phone and heard his question, but he'd pretended not to hear and hung up.

That made two! Now he had only to finish shaving and get dressed. He had just called room service for his breakfast when there was a knock at the door.

It was Dexter. A Dexter whom Maigret, albeit increasingly familiar with this phenomenon, stared at appalled.

Never in his life had he seen a man that pale and so like a sleepwalker set adrift in broad daylight in New York.

The clown was not drunk. Besides, he did not have the weepy expression of his drunken periods. On the contrary, he seemed self-possessed, but in a peculiar way.

To be precise, standing there in the doorway, he looked like those actors in comic films who have just been clubbed on the head yet remain on their feet for a moment, staring in a daze, before collapsing.

'Inspector . . .' he began, speaking with some difficulty.

'Come in and close the door.'

Then Maigret understood that the man was not drunk, but suffering from a colossal hangover. He remained upright only through a miracle. The slightest movement must have set his brain pitching and rolling, as his face convulsed with pain and his hands groped automatically for the support of the table.

'Sit down!'

Dexter brushed the idea away. Had he sat down, mightn't he have lapsed into a coma?

'Inspector, I am a lousy bum.'

As he spoke, his trembling hand had dug around in his jacket pocket and now placed on the table some folded bills, American banknotes that the inspector stared at in astonishment.

'There are five hundred dollars here.'

'I don't understand.'

'Five fat hundred-dollar bills. Brand-new. They aren't counterfeit, don't worry. This is the first time in my life I have had five hundred dollars to my name all at one time. Do you understand that? *Five hundred dollars all at one time in my pocket.*'

The waiter entered with a tray bearing coffee, bacon, eggs, jam. And morbidly hungry Dexter, who had always been ravenous in the way he had always longed to have

five hundred dollars at one time – Dexter became nause-
ated at the sight of food and the smell of bacon and eggs.
He looked away, as if about to vomit.

'Don't you want to drink something?'

'Water.'

He drank two, three, four glasses without catching his
breath.

'Forgive me. Afterwards I'll go to bed. First I had to
come and see you.'

His pale brow was beaded with sweat and he clung to
the table, which did not prevent his tall, thin body from
swaying uncontrollably.

'You can tell O'Brien, who has always thought of me as
an honest man and who recommended me to you, that
Dexter is a lousy bum.'

He pushed the money towards Maigret.

'Take this. Do whatever you want with it. It doesn't
belong to me. Last night . . . last night . . .'

He seemed to be collecting himself before tackling the
hardest part.

'. . . last night I betrayed you for five hundred dollars.'

Telephone.

'Hello! . . . What? You're downstairs? Come up, lieutenant. I'm not alone, but that's not important.'

And the clown asked, smiling bitterly, 'The police?'

'Don't be afraid. You can talk in front of Lieutenant
Lewis. He's a friend of O'Brien.'

'They can do what they want with me. I don't care. Only,
I'd like it to be quick.'

He stood there, literally oscillating like a pendulum.

'Come in, lieutenant. I'm pleased to meet you. Do you know Dexter? No matter, O'Brien knows him. I believe he has some very interesting things to tell me. Would you take a seat in that armchair while he talks and I have my breakfast?'

The room was almost cheerful, thanks to the sunshine slanting through it in a glistening swarm of golden dust.

Maigret, however, was wondering if he had done the right thing in asking the lieutenant to hear what Dexter would say. O'Brien hadn't lied in saying the previous evening that Lewis was as unlike him as possible.

'Delighted to make your acquaintance, inspector.'

Only, he said it without smiling. Clearly on duty, he sat down in an armchair, crossed his legs, lit a cigarette and, before Dexter had even opened his mouth, was already pulling a notebook and pencil from his pocket.

He was of middling height, a little below average weight, with an intellectual's face, like a professor's, for example: long nose, glasses with thick lenses.

'You can take down my statement, if necessary,' Dexter intoned, as if seeing himself already condemned to death.

And the lieutenant, immobile, observed him with cold eyes, his pencil poised for action.

'It was perhaps eleven at night. I don't know. Maybe around midnight. Over by City Hall. But I wasn't drunk, and you can believe me.

'Two men came over to lean on the bar next to me and I knew right away it was on purpose, they'd been looking for me.'

'Would you recognize them?' the lieutenant asked.

Dexter looked at him, then at Maigret, as if asking him to whom he should be speaking.

'They were looking for me. There are things you just know. I had the feeling they were part of the gang.'

'What gang?'

'I am very tired,' Dexter said carefully. 'If I am interrupted all the time . . .'

And Maigret could not help smiling as he ate his eggs.

'They offered me something to drink, and I knew it was to worm out information. You see, I'm not trying to lie or make excuses. I also knew that if I drank, I was done for, and yet I didn't refuse the scotches, four or five, I can't remember now.

'They called me Ronald, even though I hadn't told them my name.

'They took me to another bar. Then to another one, but this time in a car. And in that bar, all three of us went upstairs to a billiard room. No one else was there.

'I was wondering if they wanted to kill me.

'"Sit down, Ronald," the biggest guy said, after locking the door. "You're a sorry bastard, aren't you? You've been a sorry bastard all your life. And if you've never been able to do anything worth doing, it's because you've always lacked the capital to get started."

'You know, inspector, how I am when I've been drinking. I told you about that myself. I should never be allowed to drink.

'I saw myself as a little kid. I saw myself through all the ages of my life, always the poor jerk, always chasing after a few dollars, and I began to cry.'

What kind of notes could Lieutenant Lewis be taking? Because now and then he would write a word or two in his notebook, listening as solemnly as if he were interrogating the most dangerous of criminals.

'Then, the bigger fellow pulled some bills from his pocket, beautiful new bills, hundred-dollar bills. There was a table with a whisky bottle and some soda water. I don't know who brought them, because I don't remember seeing a waiter come in.

'So he tells me, "Drink, you idiot."

'And I did. Then he folded the bills, after counting them in front of me, and stuffed them in the outside pocket of my jacket.

'"You see, we're being nice to you. We could have got you a different way, by scaring you, because you're a scaredy-cat. But poor saps like you, we'd rather buy you. Get it?

'"And now, spill it! You're going to tell us everything you know. Everything, you understand?"'

The clown looked at the inspector with his pale eyes and said distinctly, 'I told everything.'

'Told what?'

'The whole truth.'

'What truth?'

'That you knew everything.'

The inspector still didn't really understand and lit his pipe, frowning thoughtfully. What he was actually debating was if he should laugh or take seriously his clown now afflicted with the worst hangover he'd ever seen in his life.

'That I knew what?'

'First off, the truth about J and J.'

'But what truth, goddammit?'

The poor fellow gaped at him in amazement, as if wondering why Maigret was suddenly pretending not to have a clue.

'That Joseph, the one with the clarinet, was the husband or lover of Jessie. You know perfectly well.'

'Really?'

'And that they had a child.'

'What?'

'Jos MacGill. I mean, look at the first name: Jos. And the dates fit. I watched you work them out yourself. Maura – Little John – was also in love with her, and jealous. He killed Joseph. Maybe he killed her afterwards. Unless she died of sorrow.'

The inspector was now staring dumbfounded at the clown. And what bewildered him the most was to see Lewis feverishly writing this down.

'Later, when Little John was making money, he felt remorseful and made provisions for the child, but without ever going to see him. Quite the opposite: he sent him off to Canada with a certain Mrs MacGill. And the boy, who'd taken the old Scotswoman's name, didn't know the identity of the person paying for his upkeep.'

'Go on,' sighed Maigret. And for the first time, he addressed Dexter with easy familiarity.

'You know the rest better than I do. I told everything. I had to earn the five hundred dollars, you understand? Because I still had some integrity left, after all.

'Little John got married, too. Anyway, he had a child whom he had brought up in Europe.

'Mrs MacGill died. Or else Jos ran away. I don't know. Perhaps you do, but you didn't tell me. Only, last night, I pretended you were sure of it.

'They kept pouring me big glasses of whisky.

'I was so ashamed of myself – you can believe me if you like – that I preferred to go right to the bitter end.

'At 169th Street there was an Italian tailor who knew all about it, who'd maybe witnessed the crime.

'And Jos MacGill wound up meeting him, I don't know how, probably by accident. And that's when he learned the truth about Little John.'

Maigret had now reached the point of blissfully smoking his pipe, like a man listening to a child tell some delightful story.

'Continue.'

'MacGill had fallen in with some unsavoury characters, like the guys from last night. And together they decided to blackmail Little John.

'And Little John became frightened.

'When they discovered that his son was coming over from Europe, they wanted to put still more pressure on the father and they kidnapped Jean Maura when the ship docked.

'I wasn't able to tell them how Jean Maura ended up back at the St Regis. Maybe Little John coughed up lots of money? Maybe, since he's pretty sharp, he learned where they were hiding his son?

'I assured them that you knew everything.'

'And that they were going to be arrested?' asked Maigret, standing up.

'I don't remember any more. I think so. And that you also knew that it was them.'

'Who, "them"?'

'The ones who gave me the five hundred dollars.'

'And that they had done what?'

'Killed old Angelino with the car. Because MacGill had learned that you were going to find out everything. There. You can arrest me.'

Maigret had to turn away to hide his smile, while the lieutenant still looked as solemn as a judge.

'What did they say to that?'

'They had me get in a car. I thought it was to go and murder me somewhere in a deserted neighbourhood. That way they could take back the five hundred dollars. They just let me out in front of City Hall and said . . .'

'Said what?'

'"Go get some sleep, idiot!" What are you going to do?'

'Tell you the same thing.'

'What?'

'I said to go get some sleep. That's all . . .'

'I assume I should never come back?'

'On the contrary.'

'You still need me?'

'I might.'

'Because, in that case . . .'

And with a longing glance at the five hundred dollars, he sighed.

'I didn't keep one cent. I won't even be able to take the

subway home. Today I'm not asking for five dollars like the other days, just one dollar. Now that I'm a lousy bum . . .'

'What do you think of all this, lieutenant?'

Instead of laughing heartily, as Maigret felt like doing, O'Brien's colleague gravely studied his notes.

'It wasn't MacGill who had Jean Maura kidnapped,' he replied.

'I should say not!'

'You know this?'

'I'm convinced of it.'

'Well, we're certain of it.'

And he seemed to be scoring a point with this distinction between American certainty and a simple French conviction.

'Young Maura was taken away by someone who gave him a letter from his father.'

'I know.'

'But we – we also know where he took the young man. To a cottage in Connecticut belonging to Maura, but in which he has not set foot for several years.'

'That's highly plausible.'

'It's certain. We have proof.'

'And it's his father who had him brought back to him at the St Regis.'

'How do you know?'

'I can guess.'

'We do not guess. The same person went back two days later to pick up young Maura.'

'Which means,' murmured Maigret, puffing on his pipe,

'that for two days there were reasons why this young man should be out of circulation.'

The lieutenant looked at him with comical astonishment.

'Coincidentally,' Maigret pointed out, 'the young man reappeared only after the death of old Angelino.'

'From which you deduce?'

'Nothing. Your colleague O'Brien will tell you that I never deduce. He will doubtless add with a touch of malice that I never think. And you, do you think?'

Maigret asked himself if he hadn't gone too far, but Lewis, after a moment's reflection, replied:

'Sometimes. When I have sufficient factors in hand.'

'By then, there's no longer any point in thinking.'

'What is your opinion of the account Ronald Dexter gave us? The name is Dexter, isn't it?'

'I have no opinion. I quite enjoyed it.'

'It is true that the dates coincide.'

'I am convinced of it. They also coincide with Maura's departure for Europe.'

'What do you mean?'

'That Jos MacGill was born one month before Little John's return from Bayonne. That on the other hand, he was born eight and a half months after his departure.'

'So?'

'So Jos MacGill could just as well be the son of either man. We have a choice, as you see. It's very useful.'

It was not Maigret's fault. The scene with the hung-over clown had put him in a good humour, and the lieutenant's cold-fish attitude was just the thing to keep him there.

'I've ordered a search through all the death certificates of that period that might pertain to Joseph Daumale and Jessie.'

And Maigret, cuttingly: 'Provided that they're dead.'

'Where would they be?'

'Where are the three hundred or so tenants who lived at that same time in the building on 169th Street?'

'If Joseph Daumale were alive . . .'

'Well?'

'He would probably have taken care of his son.'

'On condition that it was his son.'

'We'd have found him somewhere in the wake of Little John.'

'Why? Just because two young people starting out in life performed a duo cabaret act, this means they're tied together for life?'

'And Jessie?'

'Mind you, I'm not saying she isn't dead, or that Daumale isn't, either. But the latter might well have kicked his bucket last year in Paris or Carpentras, and the former could now be parked in an old ladies' home. This other case is just as possible.'

'I suppose, inspector, that you're joking?'

'Barely.'

'Follow my reasoning.'

'Then you have been reasoning?'

'All night long. We have, to start with, now twenty-eight years ago exactly, three people.'

'The three Js.'

'Pardon?'

'I said: the three Js. That's what we call them.'

'Who besides you?'

'The medium and the retired circus man.'

'By the way, I'm having them watched, as you requested. So far, nothing has happened.'

'Or will happen, probably, now that the clown has betrayed me, as he puts it. We were up to the three Js: Joachim, Joseph, Jessie. Twenty-eight years ago, as you say, there were those three, and a fourth who in this life was called Angelino Giacomi.'

'Correct.'

He started taking notes again. It was a mania.

'And today—'

'Today,' the American hastily interrupted, 'we find ourselves again looking at three individuals.'

'But they are no longer the same ones. Joachim, first, who with time has become Little John. MacGill. And another young man, who seems incontestably to be Maura's son. The fourth individual, Angelino, existed as recently as two days ago, but, doubtless to simplify the problem, he was eliminated.'

'To simplify the problem?'

'Let me rephrase that . . . Three people twenty-eight years ago and three people today. In other words, the two gone missing from the first team have been replaced.'

'And Maura seems to live in terror of his so-called secretary, MacGill.'

'You think so?'

'O'Brien told me that this was your impression as well.'

'I believe I told him that MacGill was extremely self-confident and often spoke for his employer.'

'It's the same thing.'

'Not exactly.'

'I had thought, coming to see you this morning, that you would tell me frankly what you made of this business. Agent O'Brien shared with me—'

'He spoke again of my impressions?'

'No, of his own. He told me that he was convinced you had an idea that might well be the right one. So I was hoping that by comparing your ideas and mine . . .'

'That we would arrive at the solution? Well, you heard my hired clown.'

'You agree with everything he said?'

'Not at all.'

'You think he's mistaken?'

'He concocted a pretty story, almost a love story. Right now Little John, MacGill and perhaps a few others must be over the moon.'

'I have proof of that.'

'Can you reveal it?'

'This morning MacGill reserved a first-class cabin on the liner sailing at four for France. In the name of Jean Maura.'

'That's only natural, don't you think? This young man, in the middle of his university studies, suddenly leaves Paris to hurry to New York, where his papa feels he has no reason to be. He is therefore sent back where he came from.'

'That's one point of view.'

'You see, my dear lieutenant, I understand your disappointment perfectly. You have been told, in error, that I am an intelligent man who, in the course of his career, has solved a certain number of criminal problems. My friend O'Brien, who is fond of irony, must have exaggerated a little. Now, in the first place, I am not intelligent.'

It was funny to see the lieutenant as vexed as if someone were making fun of him, when Maigret had never been more sincere.

'In the second place, I try never to form an idea about a case before it's closed. Are you married?'

'Of course,' replied Lewis, disconcerted by such a bizarre question.

'For years now, no doubt. And I'm sure you're convinced that your wife does not always understand you.'

'Sometimes, in fact . . .'

'And your wife, for her part, has the same conviction about you. Yet you live together, you spend evenings together, you sleep in the same bed, you have children . . . Two weeks ago, I had never heard of Jean Maura or Little John. Four days ago, I did not even know that Jos MacGill existed, and it was only yesterday, in the home of a helpless old gentleman, that a medium spoke to me about a certain Jessie.

'And you would like me to have a definite idea about each of them?

'I'm at sea, lieutenant . . . We probably both are. Except that you, you fight the waves, you mean to go in a definite direction, whereas I let myself drift with the current, clutching here and there on a passing branch.

'I'm waiting for some cables from France. O'Brien must have mentioned them to you. I also await, like you, the results of the research your men have undertaken in such records as death certificates, marriage licences, etc.

'Meanwhile, I know nothing.

'By the way, what time was it again that the ship leaves for France?'

'You want to sail on it?'

'Not at all, although that would be the wisest course. But the weather is lovely. This is my first sunny day in New York. It would be a pleasant walk to go and see Jean Maura off, and I wouldn't mind shaking hands with the boy, with whom I had the pleasure of making a most enjoyable crossing.'

He stood up and looked around for his hat and overcoat, while Lewis, disappointed, closed his notebook with regret and slipped it in his pocket.

'Shall we go and have a drink?' the inspector suggested.

'No offence, but I never drink spirits.'

A tiny twinkle in Maigret's wide eyes. He almost remarked, but caught himself in time: *I would have bet on it!*

They left the hotel together.

'Look! My Sicilian is no longer at his post. They must think, now Dexter has turned informer, that they don't need to keep an eye on my doings any more.'

'I have my car, inspector. Shall I drop you somewhere?'

'No, thank you.'

He felt like walking. He reached Broadway with no trouble, then the street where he hoped to find the Donkey

Bar again. After some confusion, he finally recognized the façade and entered to find the place almost deserted at that hour.

At one end of the bar, however, the journalist with the yellow teeth with whom MacGill and the boxer-detective had talked that first day was busy writing an article while nursing a double whisky.

Looking up, he recognized Maigret, made an unpleasant face but in the end nodded in greeting.

'A beer!' ordered the inspector, because the air smelled already of spring, and that made him thirsty.

He savoured it peacefully, like a man who has before him long hours of strolling around the city.

8.

At Quai des Orfèvres, as recently as a year earlier, at such moments everyone said, 'Here we go . . . The chief is in a trance.'

And cheeky Inspector Torrence, who in fact worshipped Maigret, used to say bluntly, 'The chief has jumped in the deep end . . .'

'In a trance' or 'in the deep end' was in any case a development the chief inspector's men welcomed with relief. They had learned to intuit its approach through small tell-tale signs and to foresee before Maigret himself when the critical moment would arrive.

What would someone like Lieutenant Lewis have thought of his French colleague during the hours that followed? He would never have understood, that's for sure, and would doubtless have pitied him, in a way. Could Agent O'Brien himself, with his fine sense of irony behind that stolid façade, have followed the inspector that far?

The change would come in a rather peculiar manner, which Maigret had never cared enough to analyse yet had learned to recognize, having heard his colleagues at the Police Judiciaire discuss it in great detail.

For days, sometimes weeks, he would flounder along in a case, doing what there was to do, no more, giving orders, gathering information about this or that person, apparently with only an average interest in the investigation and sometimes none at all.

The reason was that throughout this period he was still seeing the problem only in a theoretical way. Some man was killed in such and such a circumstance. Whosis and So-and-so are suspects.

Those people, deep down, did not interest him. *Did not interest him yet.*

Then suddenly, when least expected, when he seemed discouraged by the complexity of his task, things would click.

Who was it who claimed that at that moment he actually became heavier? Wasn't it a former commissioner of the Police Judiciaire who had watched him work for years? The remark was only a joke, but it was the truth. Maigret, suddenly, would appear weightier, more compact. He'd have a different way of gripping his pipe between his teeth, of smoking it in short, widely spaced puffs, of looking around him almost furtively, when in reality he was completely absorbed in his thinking.

It meant, in short, that the characters in the drama had just ceased to be things, pawns, puppets and had become human beings.

And Maigret put himself in their place. He struggled to get inside their skin.

Whatever a fellow human being had thought, lived, suffered, was he not capable of thinking, reliving, suffering it as well?

An individual, at a certain moment in his life, in particular circumstances, had reacted . . . Now the inspector had essentially to put himself in the other's place and thereby experience the same reaction.

Only, it was not a conscious effort. Maigret was not always aware of it. For example, he thought he was still Maigret and thoroughly Maigret while he ate lunch alone at a counter.

Yet had he looked in the mirror, he would have noticed some of Little John's expressions. Among others, the one on the former violinist's face in the St Regis when, having come unseen from the far end of his apartment, from that austere room he had arranged as a kind of refuge, he had first caught sight of the inspector through that half-open door.

Was it fear? Or in a way, an acceptance of his fate?

That same Little John, walking to the window in difficult moments, drawing aside the curtain with a nervous hand and gazing outside, while MacGill automatically took charge of the situation . . .

It was not enough to decide, 'Little John is this or that . . .'

One had to feel it, to become Little John. And that is why, as he walked through the streets, as he hailed a taxi for the passenger ship terminal, the outside world did not exist.

There was the Little John of long ago, who had arrived from France on the *Acquitaine* with his violin under his arm, along with Joseph the clarinettist.

The Little John who, during his miserable theatrical tour of the American South, shared his dinner with a thin, sickly girl, this Jessie nourished on bits of the two men's meals.

Maigret barely noticed the two policemen he recognized on the boarding dock. He smiled vaguely. Clearly Lieutenant Lewis had sent them just in case; he was doing his job properly, so he could not be faulted for that.

Only fifteen minutes before departure time, a long limousine pulled up in front of the customs buildings. MacGill jumped out first, then Jean Maura, in a light-coloured tweed suit he must have purchased in New York, and lastly Little John, who appeared to have definitively restricted his clothing to black or navy blue.

Maigret did not hide. The three men had to pass close to him. Their reactions differed. MacGill, walking ahead with Jean's light travel bag, frowned and then, perhaps out of bravado, put on a bit of a sneer.

Jean Maura hesitated, looked at his father, stepped over to the inspector and shook his hand.

'You're not sailing for France? . . . Once again, I apologize . . . You should have taken the boat with me. It was all nothing, you know . . . I behaved like a fool.'

'It's all right.'

'Thank you, inspector.'

As for Little John, he kept walking and waited a little farther on, then nodded slightly, discreetly, to Maigret.

The inspector had seen him only in his apartment. Outdoors, rather to his surprise, Maigret found him even shorter than he had thought. And older, more careworn. Was that a recent development? A pall seemed to hang over the man, yet one could still feel his extraordinary energy.

None of those things mattered. They were not even

thoughts. The last passengers were embarking. Relatives and friends remained lined up along the pier, looking upwards. A few of them, English, threw their customary coloured paper streamers up at the rails, where passengers caught and held the ends with solemn faces.

The inspector spotted Jean Maura on the first-class gangway. He viewed him from below and for an instant thought he saw, not the son, but the father; he felt that he was watching not that day's sailing, but the one so long ago, when Joachim Maura had returned to France, where he would remain for almost ten months.

And Joachim Maura had not travelled first class, but third. Had he come alone to the ship? Had there not been, for him as well, two people on the pier?

Maigret looked reflexively around for them, imagining the clarinettist and Jessie, who must have waited as he did, gazing upwards, to see the moving wall of the ship pull away from the pier.

Then... Then the both of them left... Did Joseph take Jessie's arm? Was it Jessie who automatically clung to Joseph's arm?... Was she crying? Did Joseph tell her, 'He'll be back soon'?

In any case, there were only the two of them then in New York, while Joachim, standing on the deck, watched America shrink and finally vanish in the evening fog.

This time as well two people remained, Little John and MacGill. They left side by side, walking evenly to their waiting car. MacGill opened the rear door, then moved aside.

One should not try to go too fast, like Lieutenant Lewis,

chasing after the truths one is hunting. It's best to let the pure and simple truth arrive on its own.

And that is why Maigret headed, hands in his pockets, for an unfamiliar neighbourhood. What did it matter . . . In his mind, he was following Jessie and Joseph into the subway. Did the subway exist back then? Probably. They must have gone straight home to the building on 169th Street. And there, had they separated on the landing? Hadn't Joseph consoled his companion?

Why did a quite recent memory now occur to the inspector? At the time, he had not paid attention . . .

At noon, he had nursed his beer for a long while at the Donkey Bar. He had ordered another, because it was good. Just as he was leaving, Parson, the journalist with the rotten teeth, had looked up and exclaimed, 'Good day to you then, Monsieur Maigret!'

But he had said it in French, with a strong accent, and had pronounced his name as 'Maygrette'. He had an unpleasant voice, too sharp and shrill, with crude, even nasty inflections.

Definitely a bitter man, a resentful troublemaker. Maigret had looked at him, a touch surprised. He'd muttered a vague 'Good day' and left, thinking no more of it.

He remembered suddenly that the first time he had gone to the Donkey Bar with MacGill and the gum-chewing detective, his name had not been mentioned. Nor had Parson said that he knew French.

It probably wasn't important. Maigret left it at that. Yet this detail filed itself away in the mass of his unconscious preoccupations.

When he found himself at Times Square, he naturally looked up at the Times Square Building, which dominated the horizon. And he recalled that Little John had his business offices in this skyscraper.

He went inside. He wasn't looking for anything in particular. But all he knew about the Little John of the present was his private residence at the St Regis. Why not take a look at this setting?

He found the Automatic Record Company in the building directory, and an express elevator whisked him to the forty-third floor.

It was without interest. There was nothing to see. All those jukeboxes, those dream-boxes found in most bars and restaurants, they led here, in the end. It was here, in any case, that those hundreds of thousands of nickels disgorged by the machines were transformed into bank accounts, share certificates, book-keeping entries.

A title on a glass door:

General Manager: John Maura

Other glass doors, numbered, bearing the names of an entire management staff and, finally, a vast room with metal desks and bluish lighting, where a good hundred men and women were busy working.

When asked what he wanted, he replied calmly, turning on his heel after knocking his pipe against it, 'Nothing.'

To take a look, quite simply. Wouldn't Lieutenant Lewis understand that?

And he walked on down the street, stopped in front of

a bar, hesitated, shrugged. Why not? It never hurt him, at such times, and he was not a weeper like Ronald Dexter. All alone at a corner of the bar, he downed two drinks in quick succession, paid and left as he had arrived.

Joseph and Jessie were on their own from then on, alone for ten months in the building at 169th Street, across from the tailor's shop.

What possessed him suddenly to say aloud, startling a passer-by, 'No . . .'

He was thinking of old Angelino, of the ignoble death of old Angelino, and he'd said no because he was sure, without knowing exactly why, that it had not happened the way Lewis had imagined.

There was something that didn't fit. He watched again as Little John and MacGill walked to the black limousine awaiting them and he repeated to himself: 'No . . .'

It had to be less complicated. Events can afford to be complicated or just seem that way. As for people, they are always simpler than one thinks.

Even a Little John . . . Even a MacGill . . .

Except that, to understand this simplicity required getting to the bottom of things, not merely skimming the surface.

'Taxi!'

Forgetting he was in New York, he began speaking French to the dumbfounded cabbie. Apologizing, he gave him Lucile's address in English.

He needed to ask her a question, only one. Like Germain, she lived in Greenwich Village, but Maigret had not expected to see such a handsome, middle-class apartment house of four storeys, with a clean, carpeted staircase and sisal mats in front of the doors.

> Madame Lucile
> Extra-Lucid Medium
> By Appointment only

He rang, and the bell sounded muffled on the other side of the door, the way it does where elderly people live. Then there were quiet footsteps, a pause and, finally, the very soft sound of a bolt cautiously withdrawn.

The door opened only a sliver; an eye peeked out at him through the gap.

Unable to keep from smiling, the inspector announced, 'It's me!'

'Oh! I'm so sorry. I hadn't recognized you. As I had no appointment scheduled, I was wondering who it could be . . . Come in . . . Forgive me for answering the door myself, but the maid is on an errand.'

There was no maid, of course, but it hardly mattered.

It was almost dark, and no lamp had been lit. Behind an armchair set before an English parlour stove, the inspector could glimpse the flickering of a coal fire.

The atmosphere was cosily warm, a touch stale. Madame Lucile was going from switch to switch, and lamps came on, their shades always of blue or pink.

'Sit down . . . Have you had any news of your brother?'

Maigret had almost forgotten that story about a brother concocted by the clown to soften up Germain and his old friend. He looked about him in amazement: instead of the bric-a-brac he had anticipated, he found a little Louis XVI sitting room that reminded him of so many others in Passy or Auteuil.

The only false note there was the old woman's excessive, clumsy make-up. Beneath a crust of cream and powder, her face was as pallid as a moon, with blood-red lips and the long bluish eyelashes of a doll.

'I've thought a lot about you and my former comrades J and J.'

'And I have a question I would like to ask you about them, madame.'

'You know, I'm almost sure . . . You remember you asked me which of the two was in love . . . I believe, now that I think about it, that they both were.'

About that, Maigret could not have cared less.

'What I would like to know, madame, is . . . Wait . . . I would like you to understand what I'm thinking here. Rarely do two young people of the same age and more or less the same background exhibit the same vitality. The same strength of character, if you prefer. There is always one who is a step ahead . . . Or we could say, one is always the leader . . . Just a moment . . .

'In that case, the second person can take various possible attitudes, depending on his temperament.

'Some accept domination by their friend, at times even welcoming it, while others constantly resist it.

'As you see, my question is rather . . . a delicate one. Take your time in answering. You lived with them for close to a year . . . Which of the two made the strongest impression on you?'

'The violinist,' she promptly replied.

'So, Joachim . . . The blond with long hair, the thin face?'

'Yes. And yet . . . He was not always nice.'

'What do you mean?'

'It's hard to explain . . . It's an impression . . . Listen: J and J were only the last act on the programme, right? Robson and I were the stars. There is a certain hierarchy in these matters. For the luggage, for example . . . Well, the violinist would never have offered to carry my suitcase for me!'

'Whereas the other man?'

'He did, several times . . . He was more polite, better mannered.'

'Joseph?'

'Yes. The one with the clarinet. Although . . . Goodness, it's hard to explain! Joachim was moody – that's what it was. He would be gracious one day, wonderfully amiable, then not say a single word to you the next day. I think he was too proud, he suffered because of his situation. Joseph, on the contrary, accepted his lot with a smile. And here I am going wrong again. Because he didn't smile very often . . .'

'Was he a sad person?'

'No, not that either! He did things correctly, decently, as best he could, no more. If you'd asked him to assist the stage hands or pop into the prompter's box he would have said yes, whereas the other one would have got his hackles up. That's what I mean. Still, I preferred Joachim, even when he was brusque.'

'Thank you.'

'Won't you have a cup of tea? Wouldn't you like me to try to help you?'

She'd spoken just then with a curious shyness, and Maigret did not understand right away.

'I could try to see . . .'

Only then did he remember that he was consulting an extra-lucid medium, and he almost – from goodness of heart, and to spare her feelings – agreed to a consultation.

But no! He could not face her playacting, that fainting voice and the questions she asked her deceased Robson.

'Some other day, madame . . . Please forgive me, but I cannot spare the time today.'

'I see . . .'

'No, really . . .'

There! He was making it worse. He truly regretted leaving her on a bad note, but he had no choice.

'I hope you will find your brother again.'

Hang on . . . When he got downstairs, a man in front of the building stood staring at him. Maigret hadn't noticed him when he arrived; one of Lewis's detectives, no doubt. Was this really still necessary?

He took another cab back to Broadway. It had already become his home port, and he was beginning to know his way around there. Why did he head straight for the Donkey Bar? First, he needed to use the phone. But above all he wanted, for no specific reason, to see that journalist with the grating voice again and knew that at this hour he would be drunk.

'Good afternoon, Monsieur Maygrette.'

Parson was not alone. He was surrounded by three or

four characters who had apparently been laughing at his witticisms for some time.

'You'll have a scotch with us, won't you?' he added in French. 'True, you don't like whisky in France. A cognac, monsieur retired detective chief inspector of the Police Judiciaire?'

He was trying to be funny. He knew – or thought – he was the centre of attention of the entire bar, where few people actually paid any attention to him at all.

'It's a beautiful country, France, isn't it?'

Maigret hesitated, postponed his phone call and bellied up to the bar next to Parson.

'You know it?'

'I lived there for two years.'

'In Paris?'

'Gay Paree, yes. And in Lille, Marseilles, Nice . . . The Côte d'Azur, right?'

He spat all that out resentfully, as if every little word meant something only he could understand.

If Dexter was a sad drunk, Parson was a mean one, and aggressive.

He knew he was ugly and scrawny, he knew he was dirty, he knew he was despised or detested and he was angry at all of humanity, which, for the moment, took the form and face of this placid Maigret looking at him with big calm eyes, the way one looks at a fly frightened by a storm.

'I bet that when you return, to your beautiful France, you'll bad-mouth America and Americans as much as you can. All the French are like that. And you'll say that New

York is full of gangsters . . . Ha! Only, you'll forget to say that most of them came from Europe . . .'

And with an ugly laugh, he pointed at Maigret's chest.

'You'll also fail to add that there are as many gangsters in Paris as here . . . Except that yours are bourgeois gangsters, with wives and children . . . and sometimes they have medals . . . Ha-ha! . . . Another round, Bob! A brandy for Mr Maygrette, who doesn't like whisky.

'But say! . . . Are you going back there, to Europe?'

He looked smugly around at his companions, really proud of having said this right to the inspector's face.

'Hey? Are you sure you'll be going back? Let's suppose the gangsters here don't want that. Huh? You think good old O'Brien or the honourable Mr Lewis will be able to do anything?'

'You weren't at the ship when Jean Maura left?' asked the inspector casually.

'There were more than enough people there without me, no? Your health, Monsieur Maygrette . . . And to the health of the Paris police.'

This last sally seemed so funny to him that he literally bent double with laughter.

'In any case, if you do take the boat home, I promise to come and ask you for an interview. "The celebrated Detective Chief Inspector Maigret has told our brilliant reporter Parson that he is quite pleased with his contacts with the Federal Bureau of Investigation and . . ."'

Two of the men with him left without a word, and, strangely enough, Parson, who saw them go, neither spoke to them nor seemed surprised.

Maigret was sorry he had no one available to tail them.

'Have another, Monsieur Maygrette . . . See, you should drink up while you can . . . Take a good look at this bar: thousands and thousands of people have propped their elbows on it as we're doing now. Some have turned down a last whisky, saying, "Tomorrow . . ."'

'And the next day, they weren't there to drink it.

'Result: one good scotch, lost. Ha! When I was in France, I always had a tag with the address of my hotel pinned in my overcoat . . . That way, people knew where to take me. You, you don't have any tag, do you?

'It's nice and practical, even for the morgue, the formalities take less time. . . Where are you going? You won't have one for the road?'

Maigret had simply had enough. He left after looking the whining journalist in the eye.

'Au revoir,' he said.

'Or adieu!' the other shot back.

Instead of phoning from the booth in the Donkey Bar, he preferred to walk back to his hotel. There was a telegram in his pigeonhole, but he did not open it before he reached his room. And even there, toying with it, in a way, he placed the envelope on the table and dialed a number.

'Hello, Lieutenant Lewis? . . . Maigret here. Have you turned up any trace of a marriage licence? . . . Yes . . . And the date? . . . One moment . . . In the name of John Maura and Jessie Dewey? . . . Yes . . . What? . . . Born in New York . . . Good . . . The date? . . . I don't quite understand . . .'

In the first place, he found it harder to understand

English on the phone than in ordinary conversation. And then, the lieutenant was explaining some complicated matters.

'Right. You say that the licence was issued at City Hall. Tell me, exactly what is that, City Hall? . . . Municipal offices? . . . Fine. Four days before Little John left for Europe . . . And then? . . . What? That doesn't prove they were married?'

That was what was confusing him.

'Yes . . . One can have a marriage licence and not use it? In that case, how can we find out if they got married? . . . Huh? Only Little John could tell us? . . . Or the witnesses, or whoever has the actual licence today . . . Things are easier back home, obviously . . . Yes . . . I don't think that is important . . . I said, I don't think that is important . . . Whether they're married or not . . . What? . . . I can assure you that I have no new information. I simply went for a walk . . . The young man said goodbye, politely . . . He added that he was sorry I was not making the return voyage with him . . .

'I suppose, now that you have Jessie's family name, you'll be able to . . . Yes . . . Your men are already on it? . . . I can't hear you very well . . . No trace yet of her death certificate? . . . That doesn't mean anything, does it . . . People don't always die in their beds . . .

'No, no, my dear Lieutenant Lewis, I am not contradicting myself. I told you this morning that people whom one cannot find have not necessarily left the living for the dead . . . I've never claimed that Jessie was still alive . . .

'One moment: will you stay on the line? I just received

a cable from France in reply to my request for information but haven't opened it yet . . . Of course not! I particularly wanted you available on the phone.'

He set down the receiver and opened the envelope. The cable was very long; the gist of it was:

Joachim-Jean-Marie Maura: born in Bayonne on . . . Son of town's chief hardware store owner. Lost mother early. Studies at lycée. Music studies. Bordeaux Conservatory. First Prize violin at nineteen. Left for Paris soon afterwards.

. . . First returned Bayonne four years later on father's death; sole heir, complicated inheritance amounting probably two or three hundred thousand francs.

. . . Cousins still in Bayonne and area claim he has made fortune in America but has never answered their letters . . .

'Are you still there, lieutenant? Forgive me for making you wait . . . Regarding Maura, nothing important here. May I keep reading? . . .'

Joseph-Ernest-Dominique Daumale, born in Bayonne on . . . Son of postmaster and schoolteacher. Mother widowed when he was fifteen. Studies at lycée, then Bordeaux Conservatory. Departure for Paris, probable reacquaintance with Maura. Long stay in America. Currently orchestra director in spa towns. Spent last season in La Bourboule; has built villa and must presently reside there. Married to Anne-Marie Penette, of Sables-d'Olonne; they have three children . . .

'Hello . . . Still there, lieutenant? . . . I can tell you that I've found one of your dead persons . . . Yes, I know they aren't yours. It's Joseph . . . Yes, the clarinet. Well, Joseph Daumale is in France, married, a father, owner of a villa, and an orchestra conductor . . . You'll continue the investigation? . . . What? . . . No, really, I assure you, I am not joking . . . I know, yes . . . Of course there is old Angelino . . . You sincerely want to . . .'

Lewis had begun speaking so animatedly at his end that a discouraged Maigret no longer tried to decipher his English but simply muttered indifferently in response.

'Yes . . . Yes . . . Suit yourself . . . Goodbye, lieutenant . . . What am I going to do? That depends on what time it is in France . . . What's that you say? Midnight? . . . That's a bit late. If I telephone from here at one in the morning it will be seven o'clock over there. By which hour people should be up when they own a villa in La Bourboule. An hour, in any case, at which they are almost certainly at home.

'Meanwhile, I shall simply go to the cinema. There must be a comedy showing somewhere on Broadway. I confess, I like only funny films.

'Goodbye, lieutenant. My regards to O'Brien.'

And he went to wash his hands, splash water on his face, brush his teeth. He placed each foot in turn on the armchair seat to clean his dusty shoes with a dirty handkerchief, which would have earned him a scolding from Madame Maigret.

After which he went briskly downstairs, pipe between his teeth, and carefully selected a nice little restaurant.

It was almost as if he were dining tête-à-tête with

himself. He ordered his favourite dishes, then an old burgundy and an Armagnac for special occasions. He hesitated between a cigar and his pipe, opting finally for his pipe, and found himself again among the moving neon signs of Broadway.

No one knew who he was, luckily, for his prestige would probably have been tarnished in American eyes. Round-shouldered, hands in his pockets, he looked like a bourgeois out-of-towner, window-shopping, allowing himself the occasional admiring glance at a pretty woman, pausing before the film posters at the cinemas.

One of them was showing a Laurel and Hardy and Maigret, satisfied, handed over some change at the cashier's window and followed the usherette into the dark theatre.

Fifteen minutes later he was laughing his head off, so gleefully and noisily that his neighbours nudged one another with their elbows.

One small disappointment, however. The usherette came to ask him politely to put out his pipe, which he shoved with regret into his pocket.

9.

After leaving the cinema, at around eleven thirty, Maigret was calm, a little sluggish, neither nervous nor tense, and this so reminded him of other investigations when, at a specific moment, he'd had the same impression of quiet strength, with at most a hint of uneasiness in the back of his throat – stage fright, essentially – that for a few moments he forgot he was on Broadway, not Boulevard des Italiens, and wondered what street to take for Quai des Orfèvres.

He began by drinking a glass of beer in a bar, not because he was thirsty but through a kind of superstition, because he had always had a beer before beginning any difficult interrogation or even during the questioning itself.

He remembered the large beers Joseph, the waiter at the Brasserie Dauphine, used to bring up to his office at Quai des Orfèvres, for him and often as well for the poor, wan fellow facing him, awaiting his questions with the near certainty of leaving that office in handcuffs.

Why, that evening, was he thinking of the longest, the most difficult of all those interrogations, the one considered almost classic in the annals of the Police Judiciaire, the interview with Mestorino, which had gone on for no less than twenty-six hours?

When it was over, the air was unbreathable, the office choked with pipe smoke and littered with ashes, empty glasses and the remains of sandwiches. The two men had removed their jackets and ties and their faces were so exhausted that anyone not knowing beforehand would have had trouble telling which one was the murderer.

Shortly before midnight, Maigret called the St Regis from a phone booth and asked for Little John's apartment.

It was MacGill's voice he recognized on the line.

'Hello . . . It's Maigret . . . I would like to speak to Mr Maura.'

Did something in his voice make clear that the time for playing cat and mouse was over? The secretary simply replied, without elaborating, with evident sincerity, that Little John was attending an event at the Waldorf and would probably not be back before two in the morning.

'Would you telephone him or, even better, go and meet him?' asked Maigret.

'I'm not alone here. I have a lady friend at the apartment and . . .'

'Send her home and do as I tell you. It is absolutely necessary, you hear me – it is essential, if you prefer – that you and Little John be in my room at the Berwick at ten minutes to one at the latest. At the latest, I insist . . . No, it is not possible to meet somewhere else. If Little John is reluctant, tell him that I want him to be present at a conversation with someone he knew a long time ago . . . No, I'm sorry, I can't say anything more at present. *Ten minutes to one.*'

He had arranged for a call to La Bourboule at one o'clock and had some time left before then. At that same tranquil pace, pipe between his teeth, he made for the Donkey Bar, which was crowded but where, to his great disappointment, he did not see Parson.

He drank another beer anyway, and that was when he noticed a small back room at the far end of the bar. He went over there. Two lovers in one corner. In another, on the black leather banquette, the journalist slumped, legs sprawled, staring vacantly at a tipped-over glass.

Although he recognized the inspector, he did not bother to move.

'Can you still hear me, Parson?' grumbled Maigret, planting himself in front of the man with perhaps as much pity as contempt.

Stirring only slightly, the other stammered in English, 'How do you do?'

'This afternoon, you spoke about conducting a sensational interview with me, didn't you. Well, if you have the courage to come with me, I believe you'll find material for the biggest scoop of your career.'

'Where do you want to take me?'

He was having trouble speaking, his gummy mouth was mangling the syllables, yet in the depths of his drunkenness he still seemed somewhat lucid, maybe even completely so. There was defiance in his eyes, perhaps fear. But his pride was stronger than his fear.

'The third degree?' he asked disdainfully,

'I won't even be questioning you. It's no longer necessary.'

Parson attempted to rise, falling back twice on the banquette before he succeeded.

'One moment,' said Maigret quickly. 'Are any of your friends in the bar right now? I mean the ones you're thinking of . . . I'm asking this for your sake. If there are any, it might be better for you if I leave first and wait for you in a taxi a hundred metres from here, to the left.'

The journalist tried to understand, and failed: his overriding concern was to avoid losing face. He looked into the other room, propping himself up against the door frame.

'Go on . . . I'll follow you.'

And Maigret did not try to determine which of the bar patrons belonged to the gang. It had nothing to do with him. That was Lieutenant Lewis's business.

Outside, he hailed a taxi, sent it to park at the prearranged place, and took a seat in the back. Five minutes later, hardly staggering at all but forced to stare straight ahead to remain upright, Parson arrived and opened the rear door.

'Taking me for a one-way ride?' he asked.

'The Berwick, please,' Maigret told the driver.

It wasn't far. The inspector helped Parson to the elevator. The man's tired eyes still held the same mix of panic and pride.

'Is Lieutenant Lewis up there?'

'Neither him nor anyone from the police.'

Maigret turned on every light in the room. Then, after seating Parson in one corner, he called room service to order a bottle of whisky, glasses, soda water and four bottles of beer. Just before hanging up, he added, 'And a couple of ham sandwiches, too.'

Not because he was hungry, but because this old habit of his at Quai des Orfèvres had become a kind of ritual.

Parson had collapsed again, as at the Donkey Bar, closing his eyes now and then, drifting briefly into a doze from which the slightest noise startled him awake.

Half past midnight. A quarter to one. The bottles, glasses and tray of sandwiches were lined up on the mantelpiece.

'Can I drink?'

'Of course. Stay there. I'll get it for you.'

Given Parson's condition, whether he was a bit more or a bit less drunk did not matter at all. Maigret poured him a whisky and soda that the man took from his hand with an astonishment he could not hide.

'You're a weird fellow. Damned if I can figure out what you intend to do with me.'

'Nothing at all.'

The telephone rang. Little John and MacGill were downstairs.

'Ask those gentlemen to come up.'

And he went to wait for them at the door. He saw them appear at the end of the corridor. Little John in evening dress, tauter and more nervous than ever; his secretary wearing a dinner jacket and a faint smile.

'Come in, please. Forgive me for having disturbed you, but I believe it was absolutely necessary.'

MacGill was the first to spot the journalist slumped in his armchair, and the start he gave did not escape Maigret.

'Pay no attention to Parson. I wanted him here for reasons that will be clear to you later. Sit down, gentlemen.

I would advise you to remove your coats, because this will doubtless take a while.'

'May I ask you, inspector—'

'No, Mr Maura. Not yet.'

And he had about him such an aura of quiet strength that the two men made no protest. Maigret had seated himself at the table on which he had set the telephone and his watch.

'Please be patient for a few more minutes. You may smoke, of course. I'm sorry that I have no cigars to offer you.'

He was not being flippant, and as the hour approached, his throat slowly tightened, and he puffed rapidly on his pipe.

In spite of all the lights, the room was rather dim, as in all third-rate hotels. In the next room, a couple could be heard getting ready for bed.

Finally, the telephone rang.

'Hello . . . Yes . . . Maigret . . . Hello, yes, I placed a call to La Bourboule . . . What? . . . I'll hold the line.'

And keeping the receiver to his ear, he turned to Maura.

'I'm sorry that your American phones don't have a second earpiece like those at home, because I would have liked you to be able to hear the entire conversation. I promise to repeat the important parts for you, word for word.

'Hello! Yes . . . What? . . . There's no answer? . . . Try again, mademoiselle. Perhaps everyone in the house is still asleep . . .'

For some unknown reason it moved him to hear the telephone operator in La Bourboule, who for her part was quite nervous about handling a call from New York.

It was seven in the morning over there. Was it sunny? Maigret remembered the post office, across from the spa on the banks of a mountain stream.

'Hello! Who is this, please? . . . Good morning, madame! . . . Forgive me for having awakened you . . . You were already up? . . . Would you be kind enough to call your husband to the phone? . . . I'm sorry, but I am calling from New York and it would be hard for me to call back in half an hour . . . Wake him up . . . Yes.'

As if out of delicacy, he avoided looking at the three men he had gathered in his room to overhear this baffling interrogation.

'Hello! Monsieur Joseph Daumale?'

Little John could not help crossing and uncrossing his legs but gave no other sign of emotion.

'Maigret speaking . . . Yes, the Maigret of the Police Judiciaire, that is correct. I hasten to add that I have retired from Quai des Orfèvres and that I am speaking to you as a private citizen . . . What? . . . Wait. First tell me where your telephone is in your house . . . Your study? Upstairs? . . . One more question. Can you be heard from downstairs or the neighbouring rooms? . . . That's right. Close the door. And if you have not already done so, put on a dressing gown.'

He would have bet that the man's study was done up in the Renaissance style, with massive and well-polished carved furniture, and that the walls were hung with photographs of the various orchestras Joseph Daumale had directed in the small casinos of France.

'Hello! Hold on while I have another word with the

operator on this line . . . Please be good enough to let us speak privately and to make sure that we are not cut off . . . Hello! Thank you . . . Are you there, Monsieur Daumale?'

Did he have a beard now, a moustache? A moustache, almost certainly. Salt and pepper, no doubt. And glasses with thick lenses. Had he had time to put them on when he jumped out of bed?

'I am going to ask you a question that will seem both absurd and indiscreet, and I ask you to think before you answer. I know that you are a person of sober habits, a responsible family man . . . What? . . . You are an honest man?'

Maigret turned to Little John to repeat, without a trace of irony, 'He says he is an honest man.'

'I do not doubt that, Monsieur Daumale,' he continued. 'Since the matter here is serious, I am confident that you will answer me frankly. When was the last time you were drunk? . . . Yes, you heard correctly . . . I said drunk. Really drunk, you understand? Drunk enough to lose your self-control.'

Silence. And Maigret imagined the Joseph of earlier times, as he had invented him while listening to Lucile sift through her memories. He must have put on some weight since then. Perhaps honoured with a decoration? . . . Could his wife be eavesdropping out on the landing? . . .

'You should make sure that no one is listening outside your door . . . What's that? . . . Yes, I'll wait.'

He heard steps, the sound of the door opening and closing.

'So! Last July? What? . . . That was only the third time in your life? I congratulate you.'

Some noise, in the hotel room, over by the mantelpiece. It was Parson, who had gone to pour himself a whisky, knocking the neck of the bottle against the glass with a hesitant hand.

'Tell me the details, will you? In July, which means in La Bourboule . . . At the casino, I thought so . . . Merely by chance, of course . . . Wait. I'll help you out here. You were with an American, weren't you, someone named Parson . . . You don't remember his name? That hardly matters. A thin, untidy fellow with whitish-blond hair and yellow teeth . . . Yes . . . What's more, he's right here with me . . . What?'

'Calm down, please. I can assure you that you will not have any difficulties because of this.

'He was at the bar . . . No. Forgive me if I repeat your responses, but certain people here with me are interested in what you have to say . . . No, no, the American police are not involved. Have no fear for your position and your family's peace of mind.'

Maigret's voice had turned contemptuous and it was almost with complicity that he glanced at Little John, listening with his forehead in one hand, while MacGill toyed nervously with his gold cigarette case.

'You have no idea how it happened? One never does in such cases. One has a drink, or two, yes . . . It had been years since you'd had any whisky? Obviously. And you were enjoying talking about New York . . . Hello! . . . Tell me, is it sunny, where you are?'

It was ridiculous, but he had been wanting to ask that question from the very beginning of the conversation. As if he needed to see this person in his setting, his own atmosphere.

'Yes, I understand. Spring comes earlier in France than it does here. You talked a lot about New York and your early life here, didn't you? J and J . . . How I learned that isn't important.

'And you asked him if he knew a certain Little John . . . You were very drunk . . . Yes, perfectly, I know he was the one making you drink. Drunks don't like to drink alone.

'You told him that Little John . . . Oh, but yes, Monsieur Daumale . . . Really, please . . . What? You don't see how I could force you to answer? Let's say, for example, that tomorrow or the next day a police inspector calls on you armed with a summons in due form to provide evidence in court . . .

'Pull yourself together, will you? You've caused a great deal of harm. Without meaning to, it's possible, but you have caused harm all the same.'

His raised his voice, furious, motioning to MacGill to pour him a beer.

'Don't tell me you don't remember. As for Parson, unfortunately, he remembered everything you said. Jessie . . . What? . . . The building on 169th Street . . . Speaking of which, I have bad news for you. Angelino is dead. He was murdered, and in the end you are the one responsible for his death.

'Stop whimpering, will you?

'That's right, sit down if your legs feel wobbly. I've got

167

time. The telephone service has been notified not to cut us off. As for who will be paying for the call, we'll see about that later. Don't worry, it won't be you . . .

'What? That's right: say anything you want, I'm listening. Just remember that I'm already well informed and it's useless for you to lie.

'You are a miserable wretch, Monsieur Daumale.

'An honest man, I know, you've already said that . . .'.

Three silent men in a dimly lit hotel room. Parson had collapsed once more into his armchair and remained there, eyes half closed, mouth half open, while Little John kept his forehead cradled in his slender white hand and MacGill poured himself a glass of whisky. The white patches of the two shirtfronts, the cuffs, the black of the tailcoat and dinner jacket, and that single voice resounding through the room, now heavy and scornful, now shaking with anger.

'Talk . . . You loved her, of course. It was hopeless . . . Naturally! . . . I tell you that I do understand and even, if you need to know, that I believe you . . . Your best friend . . . Given your life for him.'

What disdain dripped from his words!

'All weaklings say that and it doesn't stop them from lashing out. I know. I know. You didn't turn on him. You simply took advantage of the situation, didn't you? . . . No, she wasn't the one . . . Do me a favour, don't insult her on top of everything. She was a little girl and you were a man.

'Yes . . . Maura's father was at death's door. I know that. And he left . . . The two of you came back to 169th Street. She was very unhappy, I can imagine . . . That he wouldn't come back? . . . Who told her that? . . . Not a chance! You're the one who put that idea into her head. It shows even in your photo from those days. That's right, I have it . . . You don't any more? Well, I'll send you a copy of it.

'Poverty? Didn't leave any money? How could he have left you any when he had no more than you did?

'Understandable. You couldn't do your duo number alone. But you could play the clarinet in cafés, cinemas, in the streets if you had to.

'You made some money that way? Good for you.

'Too bad you made something else, too. Love, I mean.

'Only, you knew perfectly well there was another love involved, two other loves, Jessie's and your friend's.

'And afterwards? Cut it short, Monsieur Daumale. Now you're writing pulp fiction.

'More than ten months, I know . . . It wasn't his fault if his father, whom they'd thought was near death, was lingering on. Or that he had difficulties later settling the estate.

'And during this time, you had replaced him.

'And when the child was born, you were so afraid – because John was saying he would soon return – that you handed him over to Child Welfare.

'What are you swearing to? . . . What? . . . You want to go and check the corridor again? . . . Be my guest. And drink a glass of water while you're at it, because I think you need it.'

It was the first time in his life that he was conducting an interrogation five thousand kilometres away, knowing almost nothing of the man he was questioning.

Perspiration was beading on his brow. He had already had two bottles of beer.

'Hello? . . . It wasn't you, I know. Will you stop telling me that it isn't your fault! You had taken his place, and he came back. And instead of telling him the truth, instead of keeping the woman you claimed to have loved, you handed her back to him, which was cowardly and vile.

'Oh yes, Joseph.

'You were a dirty little coward. A lousy, gutless cheat.

'And you didn't dare tell him a child had been born. What are you saying?

'That he wouldn't have believed the child was his? Wait while I repeat your words: *John wouldn't have believed the child was his.*

'So, you, you knew that it wasn't yours . . . What? Otherwise, you wouldn't have left it with Child Welfare? And you can stand there and tell me that? . . . I forbid you to hang up, you hear? I can have you behind bars by this evening. Right!

'Maybe you became an honest man or something that looks on the outside like an honest man but back then you were a nasty piece of work.

'And all three of you continued to live on the same floor.

'John took back the place you'd taken while he was gone.

'Speak louder. I don't want to lose a word . . . John wasn't the same any more? What do you mean? . . . He was tense, worried, suspicious? Admit it – he had good reason to be! . . . And Jessie wanted to tell him everything? Good Lord, that would have been better for her, isn't that so?

'Well no, obviously, you couldn't have known beforehand. You kept her from telling him.

'And John was wondering what it was that seemed wrong all around him . . . What? She used to cry at the drop of a hat? I like that. You've got a way with words. *She used to cry at the drop of a hat.*

'How did he find out?'

Little John made as if to speak, but the inspector signalled him to be silent.

'Let him talk! . . . No, I wasn't speaking to you. You'll find out soon enough . . . He found a bill from the midwife? . . . That's true, it is hard to think of everything . . . He didn't believe it was his?

'Put yourself in his place . . . Especially handed over to Child Welfare.

'Where were you during this scene? . . . Well, yes, since you heard everything. Behind the connecting door, yes. Because there was a door between the two rooms! And for . . . for how long, in fact? . . . Three weeks . . . for three weeks after his return, you slept in that room, next to the one where John and Jessie, Jessie who had been yours for months . . .

'Finish up quickly, can you? . . . I'm sure you're not a pretty sight right now, Monsieur Daumale . . . I'm not sorry any more to be questioning you over the phone, because I think if I were there I'd find it hard to keep from punching you in the face.

'Be quiet! Just answer my questions. You were behind the door.

'Yes . . . Yes . . . Yes . . . Go on . . .'

He was staring at the tablecloth in front of him, no longer repeating what he heard. So tightly were his jaws clenched that his pipe stem finally snapped.

'And after that? Get on with it, dammit! . . . What? . . . And you didn't intervene sooner? . . . Liable to do anything, yes! . . . Put yourself in his place – or, rather, no, you couldn't . . . On the stairs . . . Angelino was delivering a suit . . . Saw everything . . . Yes.

'Well, no: you're lying again. You did not try to enter the room, you tried to get away. Only, since the door was open . . . That's right. He saw you.

'I'm not surprised that it was too late!

'This time, I have no trouble believing you. I'm sure you didn't tell Parson that. Because you could have been accused of complicity, couldn't you! And remember, you still can be . . . No, there is no statute of limitations, you're wrong . . . I can just see the wicker trunk. And the rest . . . Thanks, I don't need to know any more. As I told you at the beginning, Parson is here . . . He's drunk, yes, as usual.

'Little John is here, too. You don't want to talk to him? I can't force you to, naturally.

'Or to MacGill, whom you so nicely sent off to Child Welfare? . . . Absolutely, he's here in my room as well.

'That's all. The smell of the coffee prepared by Madame Daumale must be wafting up to you. You'll be able to hang up, heave a great sigh of relief and go downstairs to breakfast with your family.

'I bet I know how you'll explain this telephone call. An American impresario who has heard of your talents as an orchestra conductor and who . . .

'Adieu, Joseph Daumale. May I never run into you, you bastard!'

And Maigret hung up, then sat still for a long time, as if drained of all energy.

No one else had moved. The inspector rose heavily, picked up the bowl of his broken pipe and set it on the table. It just happened to be the pipe he'd bought on his second day in New York. He went to fetch another pipe from the pocket of his overcoat, filled it, lit it and poured himself a drink, not beer any more, which now seemed too bland, but a big glass of straight whisky.

'And that's that!' he sighed at last.

Little John still hadn't moved, and it was Maigret who poured him a drink and placed it within his reach.

Only after Maura had sipped from his glass and sat up a little straighter did the inspector speak again, in his normal voice, which suddenly sounded strange.

'Perhaps we'd best first finish up with that one,' he said, pointing at Parson, who was mopping his brow in the depth of his armchair.

Another weakling, another coward, but of the worst kind, the aggressive kind. Yet in fact, didn't Maigret prefer even that to the prudent and bourgeois cowardice of a Daumale?

Parson's story was easy to reconstruct. He knew, from the Donkey Bar or elsewhere, some gangsters who could use the information he'd chanced upon during his trip to Europe.

'How much did you get?' Maigret asked him wearily.

'What's that to you? You'd be only too happy to know I'd been swindled.'

'A few hundred dollars?'

'Barely.'

Then the inspector pulled his cheque from his pocket, the cheque for two thousand dollars that MacGill had given him from Little John. He took a pen from the table, endorsed the check over to Parson.

'This will be enough for you to disappear while there's still time. I needed to have you on hand in case Daumale had refused to talk, or in case I had been mistaken. You shouldn't have mentioned your trip to France, you see. I would have found out anyway, in the end, perhaps much later, because I was aware that you knew MacGill and that you also frequented those people who killed Angelino. You'll note that I'm not even asking you for their names.'

'Jos knows them just as well as I do.'

'True enough. That's none of my affair. What I am trying to spare you, I don't know why, perhaps out of pity, is having you appear before a jury.'

'I'd shoot myself first!'

'Why?'

'Because of a certain person.'

It sounded like sentimental slop, and yet Maigret would have bet that Parson meant his mother.

'I don't think it would be safe for you to leave the hotel now. Your friends certainly think that you've turned snitch, and in your crowd that's not good. I'll call downstairs to get you a room near mine.'

'I'm not afraid.'

'I'd rather nothing happened to you tonight.'

Parson shrugged, swigged some whisky straight from the bottle.

'Don't worry about me.'

He took the cheque and staggered towards the door, where he turned around.

'So long, Jos!'

And then his attempt at a parting shot: 'Bye-bye, Mister Maygrette . . .'

Presentiment? The inspector almost called him back to make him stay the night at the hotel, locking him in a room if necessary. He did not. But he could not keep from going over to the window, where he pulled aside the curtain in a gesture typical not of him, but of Little John.

A few minutes later came some muffled detonations: an unmistakeable burst of machine-gun fire.

And Maigret, walking back towards MacGill and Little John, heaved a sigh.

'I don't think it's any use going down. They've put paid to him!'

10.

They stayed for another hour in the room, which gradually filled, as at the office at Quai des Orfèvres, with the smoke of pipes and cigarettes.

'I apologize,' Little John began by saying, 'for the way my son and I tried to brush you off.'

He was tired, too, but now seemed to experience a great release, an infinite, almost physical relief.

For the first time since Maigret had met him, gone was the tension of a man coiled up within himself, striving painfully to keep from striking out.

'For six months now I've been holding my own against them, or, rather, giving ground only bit by bit. There are four, two are Sicilian.'

'That aspect of the case does not concern me,' Maigret observed.

'I know. Yesterday, when you came to the hotel, I almost spoke to you, and Jos stopped me.'

His face hardened, his eyes became more inhuman than ever, but now Maigret knew what suffering gave them that dreadful coldness.

'Can you imagine,' said Little John in a low voice, 'what it's like to have a son whose mother you have killed, and still to love her?'

MacGill had gone quietly to sit in the corner armchair, the one Parson had used, as far from the two men as possible.

'I won't tell you about what happened back then. I'm not trying to excuse myself. I want none of that. You understand? I am not Joseph Daumale. He's the one I should have killed. Still, it's important that you know . . .'

'I know.'

'That I loved, that I still love the way I believe no man has loved. Faced with the collapse of everything, I . . . No, it's no use.'

And Maigret repeated gravely, 'It's no use.'

'I believe I've paid more dearly than man's justice would ever have cost me. A short while ago you stopped Daumale from going all the way to the end. I think, inspector, that you trust what I say?'

And Maigret nodded, twice.

'I wanted to disappear with her. Then I decided to accuse myself . . . He's the one who prevented me, he was afraid of getting mixed up in an ugly scandal.'

'I understand.'

'He's the one who fetched the wicker trunk from his room. He said we ought to throw it in the river. I couldn't do it. There's one thing you could not possibly have guessed. Angelino had come over. He had seen. He knew. He could tell the police. Joseph insisted that we had to leave immediately. Well, for two days . . .'

'Yes. You kept her.'

'And Angelino didn't talk. And Joseph was half mad

with fury. And I was in such a state that I could endure his presence and gave him the last of my money to do what needed to be done.

'He bought a second-hand truck. We pretended to move out and loaded everything we owned . . .

'We drove fifty miles out into the countryside, and I was the one, in a wood near the river . . .'

MacGill's voice, pleading: 'Father, be quiet . . .'

'That's all. I say that I have paid, paid in every possible way. Even through doubt. And that was the most dreadful. Because for months, I continued to doubt, to tell myself that maybe the child wasn't mine, that Jessie might have lied to me.

'I entrusted him to an honest woman I knew and I didn't want to see him . . . Even later, I felt I had no right to see him . . . You haven't the right to see the son of the . . .

'Could I have told you all that when Jean brought you over to New York?

'He is my son too.

'But he is not Jessie's son.

'I admit, inspector, and Jos knows this, that after a few years I hoped to again become a man like any other instead of a kind of automaton.

'I married . . . Without love . . . As if taking medicine . . . I had a child . . . And I was never able to live with the mother. She's still alive . . . She is the one who asked for a divorce. She's somewhere down in South America, where she has made a new life for herself.

'You know that Jos disappeared when he was around twenty . . . He was in Montreal, involved with a milieu rather like – on a lesser scale – the one where you found Parson.

'Old Mrs MacGill died . . . I lost track of Jos and never suspected that he was living so close by, at Broadway, among those people you know about.

'My other son, Jean, as he admitted to me, has shown you the letters I sent him, and you must have been surprised . . .

'You understand, it was because all I could think of was the other one, Jessie's son . . .

'I forced myself to love Jean . . . I did this with a kind of rage . . . Whatever the cost, I wanted to give him an affection that, deep inside, I felt for another . . .

'And one day, about six months ago, I saw this boy appear.'

What infinite tenderness when he said the word *boy*, when he gestured towards Jos MacGill!

'He had just learned the truth from Parson and his friends. I remember his first words when we found ourselves face to face: "Sir, you are my father . . ."'

And at that moment, MacGill begged him, 'Papa, be quiet!'

'I am being quiet. I am saying only what is necessary . . . Since then, we live together, we are working together to save what can be saved, and that explains the transfers of funds Monsieur d'Hoquélus mentioned to you . . . Because I felt that sooner or later catastrophe was inevitable. Our enemies, who had been Jos's friends, were entirely without scruples and, when you arrived, it was one of them, Bill, who put on quite an act to deceive you.

'You thought that Bill took orders from us, when we were following his . . . But you could not be persuaded to leave.

'They killed Angelino because of you, because they felt you were on the right track and they did not want to be done out of their biggest haul . . .

'I'm worth three million dollars, inspector. In six months, I've given up half a million, but they want it all.

'Go explain that to the FBI.'

Why was Maigret thinking at that very moment of his melancholy clown? It was Dexter, much more than Maura, who suddenly took on a symbolic aura, Dexter and, strangely enough, Parson, who had just got himself shot down in the street right after he had finally, and almost honestly, come into two thousand dollars.

Ronald Dexter, in the inspector's eyes, embodied all the bad luck, hardship and sorrow that can burden humanity. Dexter, who had also been paid a small fortune, and who had come to leave the five hundred dollars on this table where the beer and whisky bottles now stood near the sandwiches no one had touched.

'You might perhaps go abroad?' suggested Maigret half-heartedly.

'No, inspector. Someone like Joseph would, but not I. I've fought on alone for almost thirty years . . . Against my worst enemy: myself and my suffering . . . I've wished a hundred times that the whole thing would crack wide open, you understand? I have really, sincerely wished to make an accounting.'

'What good would that do?'

And what Little John said truly expressed his deepest thought, now that he had allowed himself to breathe again.

'It would let me rest . . .'

'Hello . . . Lieutenant Lewis?'

Maigret, alone in his room at five in the morning, had called the lieutenant at his home.

'Do you have some news?' he asked the inspector. 'A crime was committed last night, not far from your hotel, in the middle of the street, and I wonder . . .'

'Parson?'

'You know?'

'It's so unimportant, in the end!'

'What's that?'

'It isn't important! He would have died anyway of cirrhosis in two or three years and would have suffered a lot more.'

'I don't understand.'

'It doesn't matter. I'm calling you, lieutenant, because I believe there's an English ship sailing for Europe tomorrow morning and I intend to be on it.'

'You know that we haven't found any death certificate in that young woman's name?'

'You aren't going to find any.'

'What?'

'Nothing . . . In short, there has been only one murder committed – pardon me, two, as of tonight! Angelino and Parson. In France, we call such things crimes of *le milieu*.'

'What milieu is that?'

'The underworld: where no one cares at all about human life.'

'I don't follow you.'

'No matter! I wanted to say goodbye to you, lieutenant, because I am going home to my house in Meung-sur-Loire, where I shall always be glad to welcome you if you ever visit our old country.'

'You're giving up?'

'Yes.'

'Discouraged?'

'No.'

'Don't take this the wrong way . . .'

'Of course not.'

'But we'll get them.'

'I am convinced of it.'

And it was true, moreover, for three days later, at sea, Maigret heard on the radio that four dangerous crooks, two of them Sicilians, had been arrested by the police for the murders of Angelino and Parson, and that their lawyer was disputing the evidence.

As the ship was about to leave, there were a few people on the pier who pretended not to know one another but were all looking in Maigret's direction.

Little John, in a dark overcoat and blue suit.

MacGill, nervously smoking cork-tipped cigarettes.

A sad-faced person who tried to slip aboard and whom the stewards treated with sovereign disdain: Ronald Dexter.

There was also a man with red hair who remained on board until the last minute and who was treated by the police with great deference.

It was Special Agent O'Brien, who also had questions to ask over a last drink at the ship's bar.

'So, you're giving up?'

He was wearing his most innocent expression, and Maigret did his best to imitate that innocence when he replied.

'As you say, O'Brien, I'm giving up.'

'Just when . . .'

'Just when certain people who have nothing interesting to say could be made to talk, but when, in the Loire Valley, it is high time to plant out melon seedlings under cloches . . . And I've become a gardener, you see.'

'Satisfied?'

'No.'

'Disappointed?'

'Not that either.'

'Stumped?'

'I don't know anything about that.'

At the moment, that still depended entirely on the Sicilians. Once in custody, they would either talk or not, to protect themselves.

In the end they would judge it more prudent and, perhaps, more profitable, not to talk.

And ten days later, Madame Maigret asked, 'Now, what exactly did you go to America for?'

'Nothing at all.'

'You didn't even bring yourself back a pipe the way I told you to do in my letter . . .'

It was his turn to play Joseph and behave like a coward.

'Over there, you see, they're much too expensive . . . and too flimsy . . .'

'You could have at least brought me back something, a souvenir, I don't know . . .'

Because of which, he allowed himself to cable Little John:

Please send phonograph.

This was all he had to show, along with a few pennies and nickels, for his trip to New York.

OTHER TITLES IN THE SERIES

MAIGRET
GEORGES SIMENON

'It was indeed Maigret who was beside him, smoking his pipe, his velvet collar upturned, his hat perched on his head. But it wasn't an enthusiastic Maigret. It wasn't even a Maigret who was sure of himself.'

Maigret's peaceful retirement in the country is interrupted when his nephew comes to him for help after being implicated in a crime he didn't commit. Soon Maigret is back in the heart of Paris, and out of place in a once-familiar world...

Translated by Ros Schwartz

A Crime in Holland

GEORGES SIMENON

'Just take a look,' Duclos said in an undertone, pointing to the scene all round them, the picture-book town, with everything in its place, like ornaments on the mantlepiece of a tidy housewife. Everyone here earns his living. Everyone's more or less content. And above all, everyone keeps his instincts under control, because that's the rule here, and a necessity if people want to live in society.'

Outsiders are viewed with suspicion in the small Dutch town of Delfzijl. Maigret, unable to speak the language and a stranger to their strict, church-going way of life, must unearth the sins at the heart of this seemingly respectable community.

Translated by Siân Reynolds